The Black Star of Kingston

The BLACK STAR of Kingston

S. D. SMITH
ILLUSTRATED BY ZACH FRANZEN

Story Warren Books
www.storywarren.com

Trade Paperback edition ISBN: 978-0-9862235-3-2
Also available in eBook

Story Warren Books,
an imprint of
Brightener Books
www.brightenerbooks.com

Cover and interior illustrations by Zach Franzen,
www.atozach.com
Cover design by Paul Boekell, www.boekell.com, &
Erin Tegeler
Map created by Will Smith

Printed in the United States of America
16 17 18 19 20   02 03 04 05 06
Manufactured by Thomson-Shore, Dexter, MI (USA); RMA12JM383, July, 2016

Story Warren Books
www.storywarren.com

For Micah
Deo adjuvante non timendum

Low Bleaks

Kingston

Ayman
Lake

Dobble's Point

Seddleton

Forsythe Longtreader's
Map of Natalia
as it pertains to the account of
The Black Star of Kingston

I remember that awful, eerie sound. It filled every rabbit with terror. Even the king seemed to tremble. But it was only the prelude to an attack that broke on us like hail, shattered us like kindling, and flung us into the depths. In the moments before they struck, I remember thinking one thing: This is the end of the world.

From the Journal of Massie Burnson,
Black Star Company

Chapter One

Whitson Mariner, king of the displaced rabbits of Golden Coast, settled his community near Ayman Lake in the lands he called Natalia. It was a welcome refuge after the bitter inland trek that followed hard on their tumultuous sea passage. For the first time since their long voyage began and they came to the shores of Natalia, Whitson thought he might, at last, have brought his community home.

They made camp. The camp became several neighborhoods. The neighborhoods began to look like a town. Whitson named the town Seddleton after brave Seddle herself, lost during the passage. Whitson married Lord Grant's daughter, Lillie, and later their son was born. They named him

9

Lander. Prince Lander grew as the town grew, and Whitson dared to be glad. He had always been wise enough to see and bold enough to act. Now he was becoming brave enough to hope. Hope grew in Natalia, like an uprooted flower finally placed in the sunlight and soil. But trouble never dies. It only lies there, sleeping lightly, prepared to roar awake at any moment.

* * *

King Whitson sat at his desk, his candle burning low and his vision blurry from endless reviews of supplies, personnel, tasks, and the never-ending list of urgent needs. Queen Lillie sat near-by, sewing at her own desk.

Whitson rubbed at his eyes and finally put down the labor manifest, sighing as he did. He dipped his pen and signed the bottom of the page, blew on it, then spread a small measure of sand on the signa-ture. He waited a moment, then

WHITSON

spilled the sand into a bin and stuffed the paper into an envelope. After closing it, he spilled candle wax onto the seal, removed his ring and stamped the wax, then blew on it. He added the letter to a pile and took up the next paper in his stack.

"And now the Widows List," he said. "Always a sad business."

"Yes," Queen Lillie answered. "But you'll be sadder still if you don't attend to that stack of papers."

"It will never end, Lillie," he said, staring up above her head at a painting of a great ship at sea. He sighed.

"Nor will my sewing," she said. "If you're going to be buried in tasks like a king, you must at least dress like one."

He laughed, rubbing his eyes again before peering down at his desk with a grimace. There was a knock at the door. He glanced at Lillie, and she gave him a rueful smile.

"Come in," he called, leaning back in his chair.

A long, lean rabbit entered and bowed.

"Ah, Walters. Please tell me you haven't brought another report for me to review."

"I haven't, Your Majesty," Walters said.

"Then you are most welcome," Whitson said. But when he saw the look on Walters' face, he frowned. "What is it?"

"It's Lord Grimble," Walters said, casting an uneasy glance at the queen.

"Of course it is," he said. "What now?"

"He's in council this moment, angling to clear-cut the northeast glade for winter fuel stocks," Walters said, uneasy. "In ... well ... in contrast—"

"It's not *contrast*, Walters," Whitson said, scowling. "It's *contradiction*. It's specifically what I said must not be done."

"Yes, sir," Walters said, nodding. He looked pained, like the awkwardness of nobles disputing was too much for him.

"Does anyone speak against him?" Queen Lillie asked, her mouth tight.

"Mother Saramack," Walters said, "and that quite boldly."

"Once again," Whitson said. "She is as determined to build as he is to destroy, though he is far from her equal. Now I feel awful for complaining about the Widows List."

"Mother Saramack would agree with you," the queen said.

12

Walters coughed.

"Thank you, Walters," Whitson said. "Let us know if Lord Grimble plans to burn down our home."

Walters bowed awkwardly and hurried out.

When he was gone, Queen Lillie spoke. "Is he insane?"

"Walters? No, he's just anxious," Whitson said.

"Grimble," she said, frowning.

"I know, dear," Whitson said, taking her hands in his. He looked around. "Is Lander with your father?"

"Yes," she said.

"Then we must talk about this," Whitson said, kneeling beside her. "The more wood we clear, the more vulnerable we are. But right now we have no real alternative. So Lord Grimble sows discord."

"But why? Why does he always feel the need to oppose you? What can he accomplish by it?"

"He's a bitter old rabbit. I think it's more about lost ambition than any real scheme he has now. He wanted to be king. He never will be. So he must oppose me at every turn."

"He must never be king."

"No. Never! I have tried to reach out to him, Lillie."

"I know. You even gave his son a command," she said. "You haven't repaid him insult for insult."

"I can't meet him on the ground he wants. I can't be seen as a petulant striver."

"No, dear," she said. "You must be what you are, a wise king."

"I don't think he will resort to anything desperate, but I want Lander to be prepared."

She glanced at the back wall, a thoughtful expression on her face. Looking back at Whitson, she nodded.

"Then we agree?" he asked.

"Yes," she said, exhaling heavily. "He's too young, of course. But perhaps it will ground him a little."

"He's a hard one to wrangle, that's for sure. He..." Whitson paused, cocking his ear. He frowned. "Did you hear..."

Queen Lillie nodded toward the side cabinet. Whitson nodded back and slowly walked over to it. He knelt before a low wooden door covered with sketches and detailed plans of ships and knocked once. After listening for a moment

14

and hearing nothing, he knocked again. This time there was a return knock from within.

Whitson opened the door. Prince Lander was squished inside, a guilty expression on his face.

"You don't fit in there quite as easily as you used to," the king said, pulling his son free.

Lander tumbled out and onto the floor at his father's feet.

"I'm sorry," he said, rubbing his knees.

"You should be, son," Whitson said, helping Lander up. "I know you're curious, but sneaking is no virtue for a king."

"It's no virtue for *any* rabbit," Queen Lillie said, eyebrow arched.

"Yes, Father," he said. "Yes, Mother."

Whitson looked at Lillie, his eyes full of questions. She nodded calmly.

"Come with me, son," the king said, crossing to his desk.

Lander ran to his father's side. "Are you going to show me maps, Father?"

"Not today, son. I want to give you something. Something heavy and lovely."

"Heavier than the wooden ship you made for me?"

15

"Something nearly as heavy as my crown," Whitson said.

Queen Lillie laid aside her sewing and stood. She came close and put her arm around Lander. "We know it isn't easy for you to be our son."

"They think it is," he said. His head went down.

"The other children?" she asked.

He nodded.

"I'm sorry," she said. She wrapped him in a hug. While Lander leaned into his mother's embrace, Whitson crossed to the back wall and pushed against one of the planks. It gave way, turning on a pivot to reveal a hollow space behind the wall. Whitson pulled a lever within, cranking it several times. As he did, another part of the wall folded in and rose, revealing a hidden chamber.

Inside were many treasures, including golden armor, elegant clothes, and several weapons. Whitson glanced at a corner where a carved box sat on an elaborate stool, an old stone sword mounted above it. He touched his ears, his eyes, and then his mouth, muttering with his head down. Smiling, he turned and tugged on a long trunk, pulling it out into the room and dragging it to his desk.

Lander turned, his eyes widening when he saw the trunk. He craned his neck and peered at the room in the wall.

"Secrets," he whispered.

"We have a few," Queen Lillie said, smiling.

"And there's one we want to share with you today," Whitson said. "Something very important."

"Yes, Father."

"This is a trunk the old king gave me. Do you remember me telling you about the old king, about your Grandfather Whit and the heroes of Golden Coast?"

"I remember it all, Father," he said. "I'm sorry I never met Grandfather Whit. Grandfather Grant says he was a great lord."

"He was a good rabbit, and a wonderful father," Whitson said. He cleared his throat.

"Grandfather Grant says we're only all alive because of how you saved everybody in your ships," Lander said.

"That's true," Queen Lillie said.

"Grandfather Grant says it was like a new leaping?"

"Well," Whitson said, raising his eyebrows, "I wouldn't go that far. But we have made our own

17

crossing. Not over a chasm, as with the old ones, but over the wide, wild sea."

"Like Flint and Fay," Lander said. "But on your ships."

Whitson smiled at his son. To him, Lander was the most miraculous result of a long series of miracles. *For you, my son, I would do as my father did on Golden Coast. I would trade my life for yours in a moment.* Whitson felt a great wave of sadness then. But it crashed, as always, on a shore of hope. At least when he looked at his son.

"I have a gift for you, Lander," Whitson said.

He opened the trunk and reached inside.

Tales of Old Natalia

Chapter Two

Fleck drove his spade into the earth, turning it over and over. He enjoyed gardening, but he missed working in the mines. He stopped digging and wiped the sweat from his eyes. Staring off at the mountains across the lake, he thought of his father.

"Hey, Blackstar," someone called.

Blackstar? Why would someone be calling me that? Then he remembered the distinct patch on his shoulder, his father's black star miner's patch. Fleck turned around to see King Whitson Mariner himself, along with Queen Lillie and Prince Lander. The prince had a little wooden boat, a perfect model of one of the ships that had brought Fleck and many others to Natalia.

Fleck knelt. "Your Majesties, Your Royal Highness," he said.

"Please stand up," King Whitson said. "We're just going down to the shore. Thank you for the hard work you're doing."

"It's an honor to serve, sir," Fleck said, getting to his feet.

"I sometimes feel that way," King Whitson said, joining hands with Queen Lillie.

"It's a lovely day, is it not?" Queen Lillie asked.

"It is, ma'am," Fleck answered.

"You were staring at the mountains across the

lake," the queen said. "Isn't it the most forbidding sight?"

"They are ominous, Your Majesty."

She nodded. "But beautiful. Beautiful and terrible."

"Yes, ma'am," Fleck agreed.

Prince Lander scrambled down to the lake's edge and plunged his boat into the water.

"He loves the water," the king said. "I suppose he comes by it honestly."

"We're all ever so glad for that, sir," Fleck said.

"Enjoy the day, Blackstar," the king said. Queen Lillie waved as they followed Lander to the shore.

"Peace and victory to Your Majesties," Fleck said, bowing again.

King Whitson saluted him, and they walked to the water's edge.

Fleck smiled and shook his head.

* * *

Fleck had been a miner on Golden Coast before the invasion and the heroic escape brought off by Whitson Mariner. Like all the others, he owed

21

King Whitson his life. There had been hundreds of miners on Golden Coast, but most of them worked in the gold mines for the landed families. That's where the money was. But his father mined coal. Coal mining was looked down on in the decades following Hanfar's Second Rush. But no matter how poorly esteemed it was, his father called it honorable work. It kept the rabbits warm in winter, and they could not have flourished without it. Many would not have survived.

Fleck had mined for nearly a year with his father. He had been only weeks away from earning his patch, the star of black symbolizing the transition from apprentice to master. But after the invasion, that had been forgotten. Like many of the old bucks, his father had bravely stayed behind to help cover the escape. He had handed Fleck his coat with the black star patch before they said their goodbyes. After all this time, he still felt his father's loss like a fresh wound.

* * *

Hours later, after the royal family had left, Fleck was still at work. Galt had come, an old friend from a miner's family like his own. They worked well together, with an ease of understanding that a long partnership brings.

"Aren't you relieved to be here, Fleck?" Galt asked, stabbing his spade into the ground.

"I am, sure," Fleck said, dropping in a handful of seeds before Galt covered the hole with the displaced earth. "But I miss the mines, and I'm uneasy about this place. I can't put my finger on it, but those mountains beyond the lake trouble me terribly."

"Can't you just enjoy the peace we have in Natalia?" Galt asked, laughing. "Do you miss the perils so much that you have to find them when they aren't even here?"

"I don't seek them, no," Fleck said. "But you may be right. It's hard to get used to peace."

"Not for everyone else. Seems you're the only one with this burden. Do you feel guilty about being safe?"

"When so many died back home? When our fathers died?"

"Yes."

Fleck sighed. "I do. Maybe it's wrong. I know they'd want us to go on with life and find joy. But I feel like we owe them something."

"What do we owe them besides being as happy as we can?" Galt asked.

"We owe them vigilance."

They worked on in silence for a few minutes, relaxed in the quiet work. Spade in and dirt out. Seeds in and dirt to cover. The wind off the lake was cool; it made the sun's heat less oppressive.

"King Whitson says this is our new home," Galt said.

"Did he say those words?" Fleck asked.

"He as much as said it. We're here, Fleck. Here to stay."

"Well, I won't feel at home in Seddleton till I know what's in those mountains across the lake. They're ominous, dark. Even the queen says so."

They *were* dark. The foothills on the other side of the lake reminded him of their old home, but the mountains beyond were enormous. Hard and stark, they split the sky with their craggy heights.

"But you still want to go over there?"

"I do," Fleck said, taking the shovel from Galt as he gazed across the water. "There might be coal."

Galt peered at the mountains. "True. And we need it. The council's been arguing about fuel for days. I heard Lord Grimble talking about it. I don't trust lords, but he's pretty convincing."

"I'm going to ask for an audience with the king," Fleck said. "Will you come with me?"

"I'll go with you to the other side, Fleck," Galt said. "But I won't go with you to see the king."

"Are you frightened?" Fleck asked, laughing.

"Of course I am," Galt said, kicking dirt at Fleck. "He's a king."

"He's only been a king for a little while," Fleck said. "And he seems—I don't know—humble."

"Kings aren't allowed to be humble," Galt said. "Lords are all the same, Fleck. They aren't like us, with their medallions and their wealth. They probably won't even let you see him."

They heard crashing in the trees beyond, and Fleck whirled around, raising his shovel to strike. Two young bucks broke through the trees, one chasing the other. "You need to relax, Fleck," Galt said. "You weren't even this jumpy your first day in the mines."

Fleck shook his head, then walked to the water's edge. He peered across the water, rubbing his chin as he stared. Galt came beside him.

"What's in those mountains, Galt?"

Tales of Old Natalia

Chapter Three

Though he was no lord, a few days later Fleck got his audience. He was admitted by two guards dressed in white, the emblem of the red diamond on their chests matching the standard that flew over the king's offices.

"Come in, Blackstar," King Whitson said, looking up from his papers.

Fleck, head down, crept a few steps into the tent and dropped to one knee. "Your Majesty," he said. "I'm so honored."

"It's my pleasure," King Whitson said. "Please, come and sit." Fleck crossed quickly, only looking up in nervous snatches, and sat down. "What's on your mind, Blackstar? I'm sorry, I don't know your real name, but the patch on your shoulder ... I

S. D. Smith

have a bad habit of giving out names with little basis. You were a master miner?"

"I was nearly, sir."

"Does it bother you, me calling you Blackstar?"

"Not a bit, sir," Fleck said. "It's my father's coat, and I wear the black star, as he did—with pride."

"He was lost, on the coast?"

"Yes, sir."

"I'm so sorry."

"Thank you, Your Majesty. And I'm ever so sorry about your own father. Lord Whit was a great rabbit."

"He was that. What was your father's name?"

"He was Jon, my lord."

"Jonson Blackstar," Whitson said. "It has a ring to it."

"He and mother named me Fleck, but I'll answer to any name that honors him."

"Is your mother among the widows?"

"I'm afraid she passed years before the trouble came, Your Majesty."

"I'm sorry to hear that."

"Thank you, sir."

"Well," King Whitson said, his eyes moving to his papers. "I'm so sorry to rush you, my good rabbit, but I'm afraid I don't have much time to spare. How might I help you today?"

"Your Majesty is kind to see me, and I won't take long. It's only that winter's coming," Fleck said.

"And we have no fuel," King Whitson said, nodding. "I know a lot of folks are agitated about that right now. I have two teams working on the problem. We have wood, and that should be enough for this winter and a few more. But the more we chop nearby, the more vulnerable we become."

"Exactly, sir," Fleck said.

"It's too bad we don't have coal here," King Whitson said, fingering the gold chain around his neck. Fleck remembered that beneath the king's shirt hung the Ruling Stone, a ruby that served as the centuries-old symbol of the sovereign's authority. He took a deep breath.

"Sir, we might have coal."

"Oh yes? Where?"

"Well, Your Majesty, it's only a hunch. But across the lake, I think the foothills might have something worth mining in them. It may be coal. If nothing else, I feel it might be important to secure an advanced position across the water as a buffer against whatever might be in those mountains."

"Have you served in the military, Blackstar?"

"No, sir," Fleck said, "but I feel as though we should all be in the military now. I think we owe it to the heroes of Golden Coast to be vigilant."

"Do you find it hard to be happy here?" King Whitson asked.

Fleck paused, then nodded. "I do. I don't mean to be ungrateful. I miss my family, and I don't want what happened to them to happen to those here, to the littles like the prince and the others."

"Is there a Mrs. Blackstar?"

"Not yet," Fleck said. "But after we're settled and I have a vocation, I'll be looking for her."

"You don't think we're settled here?"

"Begging Your Majesty's pardon," Fleck said, "but I don't think we ought to be. Not yet."

The king paused, scratching his chin. "So, you want to go across the lake?" he asked. "How on earth could we get there? It would be a long trek, and everyone is weary of trekking."

Fleck smiled and pointed to the papers on King Whitson's desk. The king smiled back, moving the documents from the top of the pile to reveal drawing after drawing of ships' plans. "I believe we are united in purpose, Captain Blackstar."

"I'm delighted to hear that, Your Majesty, but I'm no captain."

"You are now. You will command a company of miners. Pick your team, no more than ten, and give the list to Lord Grant for approval. You will train them and help me build a ship. We will attempt to secure a working settlement on the far side of the lake and, hopefully, a mine."

"But sir," Fleck said, "there are so many more qualified rabbits—"

Whitson held up a hand. "Then why aren't they here? Why have they not come to me with passion, with a plan? I have not been a king long, but I know a leader when I see one. Captain Blackstar, gather your team."

"As you wish, lord," Fleck said. He bowed low, in part for respect and in part to hide the smile that bloomed on his face.

* * *

So Fleck formed Black Star Company. He chose Galt as his lieutenant and Burnley, a veteran of the mines, as a second. To this leadership team they added seven younger bucks, all eager and brave. Fleck secured swords for each member of the company, and they began training together daily. They also helped build the king's ship, *Vanguard*. Two additional ships were being built by the time *Vanguard* was finally finished. As the day of departure approached, they secured all the necessary mining supplies: pickaxes, candles, shovels, wheelbarrows, and even a few barrels of blastpowder. Finally, the voyage was given a complement of soldiers, led by Captain Vance. As the red sun set on the eve of the voyage, Fleck sat on the shore with Galt.

"Rumor has it that most of the court doesn't approve of the king's plan," Galt said. "They think it's mad to follow the advice of a peasant farmer whose claim

BLACKSTAR

32

to fame back on Golden Coast was that he was *almost* a coal miner."

"I do lack certain credentials," Fleck said.

"But what you don't lack is courage and vision," Galt said. "And, let's be honest, a good dose of madness."

"We go," Fleck said, gazing across the glimmering water, "mad as it may be."

"By the leapers," Galt said, "we go."

"To adventure," Fleck said, raising his waterskin.

"To madness," Galt said, knocking his own waterskin against Fleck's.

"To another crossing," Fleck said, "come what may."

Tales of Old Natalia

Chapter Four

The sails caught the wind, driving *Vanguard* forward. "Glorious, Blackstar, is it not?" King Whitson said. The three-masted ship moved out of the bay, beyond Dobble's Point and out into the wide lake. The king and Fleck stood on the command deck, a raised platform, high above which flew Whitson's standard: a red diamond surrounded by lines of gold, blue, and green. It was his own variation on the red-diamond theme of so many kings in the long history of Golden Coast.

"It's a lovely ship, Your Majesty," Fleck said. "If I may say so, it seems an improvement over the old flagship."

"It is, true enough," the king said, grinning wide. "The waves were terrific on the sea, so there's far less to worry about here. But it's a grander boat, for certain. How it glides along!"

"Will Your Majesty excuse me?" Fleck asked, bowing quickly. The king nodded, and Fleck hurried down the short ladder to the main deck. "Gavin!" he shouted. "What are you doing?"

The startled rabbit turned, saw his captain, saluted, and looked around nervously. "Uh, nothing, sir."

"Then what are you *not* doing?" Fleck asked, his face hard set.

"I don't know, sir," Gavin said, looking back and forth for salvation.

"Your duty, buck!" Fleck shouted. "This is the king's ship, you are a subject, and you are in Black Star Company. What does it mean to be in this company?"

"We protect the king and all that the king loves," Gavin called back, his voice cracking.

"What is our vow," Fleck asked, raising his voice, "to the king and to each other?"

Then all the rabbits marked with a black star shouted in unison, "My place beside you! My blood for yours!"

The sailors had continued their work during

this confrontation, at least pretending not to watch. But as Black Star Company shouted their vow, they all stopped, stood a little taller, and watched openly. The soldiers did the same, and the king himself came to the rail and watched. No one spoke.

Fleck quickly stepped closer to Gavin. King Whitson frowned. Fleck's hand shot out toward Gavin, and a loud gasp sounded from every watching rabbit. The hand stopped and wrapped behind Gavin's neck, pulling his head gently to Fleck's own so that their foreheads touched. "My place beside *you*. My blood for *yours*. We are in this together, my friend. As you are bound to me, I am bound to you. So long as you remain loyal to the king, I am loyal to you. I am on your side. I am a brother to you. Understand?"

"Understood, sir," Gavin whispered.

"Good," Fleck said, pointing to the sword at Gavin's side. "Remember your duty. We may find pleasure in our duty, but our duty is not our own pleasure."

Fleck turned and walked back toward the command deck as the ship came to life again.

Gavin sprang into action. He reported to Galt and, hearing his instruction, disappeared below deck to sort the supplies along with Massie and Kay Jack.

"My apologies, Your Majesty," Fleck said, returning to his side on the command deck.

"You are harsh, Captain Blackstar," King Whitson said, "but also tender."

"I would be happy to take either orders or suggestions, Your Majesty, on how to lead young bucks most effectively," Fleck said. "I seek vigilance above all else. It keeps rabbits alive in the mines and, I believe, on the battlefield. I want my bucks prepared for both."

"Carry on, Captain," King Whitson said, smiling as *Vanguard* cut through the low waves, sending up a spray. "I haven't been this happy in a long time. I shall have to bring Lander next time."

Fleck frowned, looking from the king to the black mountains ahead.

* * *

When they drew near to the other side of Ayman Lake, King Whitson commanded the mainsails be taken in and the anchor heaved over.

"I'll be nearby, Captain," Whitson said. "I shall take *Vanguard* to explore the mouth of the west river. But I won't be long. I can always explore it further when we have our mine working."

"I hope so, Your Majesty," Fleck said, bowing.

"Good luck, Blackstar," Whitson said. "I'll be back for you soon."

Fleck led his company over the side, into the shallow water, and then onto the pebbled shore. The soldiers followed behind.

"Be alert, bucks," Fleck said, eyes on the tangled trees ahead.

"We're tight enough to play music on," Galt said, and a few of the bucks laughed.

"I hope it isn't a tragic ballad played on our bones," Fleck said.

Galt lowered his voice. "Try not to overwhelm us with your optimism, Fleck." Then louder, to the company, he said, "Stay sharp, lads."

Fleck smiled, but he never took his eyes off the thick band of trees and brush ahead. Beyond, the foothills rose steadily to those impossibly high mountains in the distance, their craggy black peaks wreathed in mist. The fog seemed to swoop down into the foothills like a gliding ghost.

"Bows at the ready," Fleck said. Instantly, five of the rabbits drew bows and nocked arrows. They

S. D. Smith

had practiced these commands over and over, and Fleck was secretly pleased at how quickly the five with bows, including young Gavin, had acted.

The soldiers behind Black Star Company looked at each other, nodding approval and showing some surprise. Their leader, Captain Vance, moved up beside Fleck. "Your rabbits are impressive, Captain."

"Thank you, Captain Vance," Fleck answered. "That means a lot."

"We are charged with following your lead. So if you need me, call out. Otherwise, I'll lead my bucks behind you in a covering position."

"Thank you, Captain," Fleck said. "If things go badly, we will rely upon your leadership and experience."

"What do you expect to happen?" Vance asked, his eyebrows raised.

"Anything."

Tales of Old Natalia

Chapter Five

Fleck was prepared for anything, but for a long time what happened was nothing. Black Star Company and its attendant soldiers reached the foothills without incident. Lugging pickaxes and packs, and with weapons ready, they trudged through the thick forest. In a few hours of tracking back and forth, they found what both Fleck and Galt believed to be a prime spot for a potential mine. Fog draped the trees surrounding a small clearing at the base of a mossy hillside.

"It might be coal," Galt said. "I wish our fathers were here."

"Me too. And for more than this," Fleck said. "But I agree." He turned to a large brown rabbit with a massive pickaxe slung over his shoulder.

"What do you say, Burnley?"

"I agree with you both," he said, scanning the ground and the rocky hillside. "It might be coal. If a few of us can dig a bit, I think we may know more in a few hours."

"That we will," Fleck said, motioning for the four rabbits who had borne pickaxes to come forward. They took off their other gear, laying their swords and packs aside.

Following Burnley's lead, they moved toward strategic positions.

"Hold on," Fleck said, crossing to where a younger rabbit, Massie, held a pickaxe poised. Smiling, Fleck extended his open hand. Massie handed him the pickaxe.

They set to work. Fleck grinned, gaining as much pleasure from the digging as King Whitson had from sailing on the lake. He threw himself into the work. All the preparation, the defensive drilling, and their part in building the ship—it was all for this.

GALT

42

After an hour, they had all taken turns tearing into the hillside. Fleck consulted with Burnley and Galt as the younger rabbits dug on.

"We look to you, Burnley," Fleck said. "Should we carry on here, blast a hole, or find another site with promise?"

"You're the captain, Fleck," Burnley said. "And it don't bother me, even if I'm older. Your dad always said you had a head for mining."

"What, hard and dark?" Galt said. "Or likely to ignite, perhaps?"

"Thank you, Burnley," Fleck said, smiling at Galt. "I will take responsibility for the decision, but I want your honest opinion on this. You have the most experience. Do you think we'll find anything here?"

Burnley looked at each hole, back up at the mountains, then at Fleck. "I do, Fleck. I'd carry on here if it were me in charge."

"Right," Fleck said. He nodded to Galt.

Galt nodded back and returned to the digging rabbits. "We carry on, lads!" he shouted. "There's something below; we just have to find it. This ain't bucks picking up pebbles. We're miners, and we go below the earth. If your face ain't murky, you ain't doing worky!"

The morning passed. As noon came on, Fleck explained their decision to Captain Vance, whose soldiers sat beneath a tree as the mist gathered in the trees around them. Then he walked back to the site. He relieved Gavin, jumping into the hole and happily laying into the wall of packed earth and rock.

"You're doing well, Gavin," Fleck called back as Gavin scrambled out of the hole. "I'm proud of you."

Gavin tried not to smile but failed. "Thank you, Captain."

The fog hung heavy, with shafts of light breaking through in hazy pillars. The air was full of the ring and shatter of pickaxes on stone. Still, everyone heard Galt cry out.

"I've hit on something!"

They all stopped, and it grew suddenly quiet. They gathered around Galt's site, and Fleck, alongside Burnley, examined what Galt held in his hands.

"Bring some water, Gavin," Fleck said, and the buck eagerly retrieved some. Everyone was smiling now. Fleck poured the water over the fistful

Galt held, revealing something black and hard. Silence fell, and even the soldiers were roused from their apathy to meander over and huddle around the site.

"More water, Gavin," Fleck said as Galt lifted the lump to what sunlight could be found. He examined it intently.

"There's a seam in here," Massie said, pointing to the wall of the shaft Galt had been digging. Fleck nodded.

"Do we have a mine?" Captain Vance asked eagerly, and all waited for Fleck's verdict. Fleck looked at Burnley with a questioning smile.

GAVIN

A wild and eerie whine invaded the silence. Loud and high, it seemed to ride along the beams of light that split the fog. The rabbits tensed. No one moved.

"What in the—" Gavin began, but Fleck silenced him with a look.

A tense silence loomed. Just

when they thought the silence would not be broken, it came again. Louder. A screeching horror. Fleck's hand went to his sword.

Tales of Old Natalia

Chapter Six

This noise wasn't a howl, the sound that so terrified them and haunted their memories of the last days of Golden Coast. This was different.

Fleck held up a hand for silence, needlessly now, for everyone was still. The piercing call seemed to ripple inside him, to brew steady terror in his guts. He didn't like to admit it, but he was almost paralyzed with fear.

"It's only the wind?" Captain Vance whispered. A question.

"Stations," Fleck commanded, keeping his voice as calm as possible. He moved then, obeying his own charge, to the edge of the fog. Alongside him stood Galt, his recovered sword poised in his filthy hands. The excitement of their discovery was forgotten, replaced by a creeping dread. On the other side of the small clearing, the guards readied bows, swords, and pikes. Shields were lifted from the wet grass, whispered orders from Captain Vance relayed. Fleck's rabbits were at least as efficient. Gavin and Massie had resumed their bows, while Burnley stood beside them with his large pickaxe ready.

The sound came again, a chilling rise and fall of high, grating music. It seemed to carry on the slight wind, then fall away. It was hard to tell where it came from. Fleck peered into the fog, squinting hard. The rabbits stepped back and forth, looked from side to side. Some of the younger rabbits moaned softly, a worried whimper escaping their mouths.

"Where is it coming from?" Galt whispered.

"I can't tell," Fleck answered. "It feels like it's all around us."

Then they heard another sound, low and close.

"That's not the wind," Burnley muttered, choking up on his pickaxe.

"Steady," Fleck said. "Circle out." Black Star Company turned out, facing the fog. Gavin and Massie stood together, bows ready. Kay Jack and Brephen stood side by side, hands shaking. Hollis and Burnley faced the foggy terror nearby. Galt stood with Fleck. The soldiers did something similar, completing a circle that surrounded the clearing. The brush bulged with fog, and they gazed into it, eyes wide and weapons ready.

The shrieking bawl sounded again, large and loud and all around them. The low sound of thrashing grew louder. Nearer.

In front of Fleck, the forest leaves and branches bobbed as the hurried crashing came ever closer. He raised his sword.

"Here!" Galt cried. The circled rabbits turned to face Fleck's side. Gavin's eyes widened in terror and he bent his bow, fingers shaking as they gripped his nocked arrow. Massie cursed and raised his own bow with a jerk. Burnley surged forward.

"Keep your places!" Fleck shouted, and Burnley retreated. "Hold the circle!"

More baneful calls. Louder and closer. Fleck glanced back at Gavin and Massie, then blinked.

Fog and brush rippled as heavy footfalls sounded. Closer. *Closer.* A figure burst through the fog.

Fleck was already moving. He lunged. Gavin, seeing the sudden break in the fog, let go his arrow. Fleck heard the flick of the arrow as he crashed into the intruder, sending him toppling to the ground. Fleck stood where the invader had been. The speeding arrow found him instead.

Fleck reeled, falling in a wild spin on top of the intruder he had replaced.

"Hold!" Galt called, a furious backward glance at Gavin. He rushed to Fleck, rolling him off the intruder.

King Whitson. It was the king who'd come crashing in.

Fleck had saved him.

"Are you okay, Blackstar?" King Whitson asked urgently. He took Fleck's motionless face in his hands. "Come on, Captain!"

Burnley came, examining the wound as the others looked for signs of life.

"He's alive," Galt said, feeling his pulse. "How's the wound?"

"It's deep, close to his heart," Burnley answered. "We need to get him out of here, fast."

Gavin began to whine, tears starting in his eyes. He moved slowly toward Fleck. Seeing the wound and the blood that soaked Captain Blackstar's side, arm, and shoulder, he staggered. Then he ran like mad for the woods. Massie tackled him before he could escape the clearing.

The eerie cry came again, but not so loudly this time. Still, the startled rabbits ducked and spun around, trying to find the source.

"Don't run, Gavin!" Massie shouted. "The

51

Captain'll be all right, and we'll make it. We have to stick together."

"I've killed him!" Gavin shouted.

"You haven't killed him," Captain Vance said, "but you might kill us all if you don't quit shouting." He examined Fleck's wound and looked at Fleck's face. "Your Majesty," he said. "We need to get back to *Vanguard*."

"Of course," King Whitson said. "I was coming to find you when I heard that noise." He looked up. "Four or five of you—Burnley, you for sure—carry Captain Blackstar. The rest form up and defend. We make for the boat with all speed. Follow me."

Captain Vance placed his rabbits, and Galt grabbed Gavin.

"Let's go!" he whispered, an angry edge to his voice.

They followed the king and Captain Vance, moving quickly, though many were exhausted. Gavin's eyes were wide, darting from Massie to Galt to the foggy wood. Massie nodded to him and kept close.

"You can't leave, Gavin," Massie whispered. "It's treason to leave when the king's in need. And you'd really be abandoning the captain then. It will be all right; just hang on a little longer."

But when Gavin met Galt's eyes, he saw in them the loathing he knew he deserved. Galt's teeth were clenched, his fury only just buried beneath a vigilant, searching stare.

Gavin was trembling. Massie struggled to keep near him and to stay alert on the march back. They made the shoreline at last and plunged into the water. Some of the hands came to meet them and helped hoist Fleck on board. Massie joined them. Gavin moved nervously forward to help. Galt stepped between him and Fleck, a look of contempt plain on his face. Gavin stepped back slowly, his head down. He turned toward the shore and ran. Finding the tree line, he disappeared into the fog.

"Gavin!" Massie shouted. "Come back!"

"I'll find him," Burnley called, breaking from the shallows and running onto the shore. Massie followed hard behind him.

"Come back!" Galt ordered. "It's too dangerous. We must get the king and Fleck back to Seddleton."

Burnley looked to the trees and back at Galt

and the ship.

"He's right," Captain Vance said. "We have to go, Your Majesty. Please."

Whitson's face told of his frustrated anger. He looked at the two rabbits on shore and shook his head. "Come back," he said. "We can't help Gavin now."

They hurried back, heads hung and hearts heavy, and boarded *Vanguard*. King Whitson ordered the ship's hands to raise the anchor and make all possible sail. He paced the command deck, eyes on the shoreline. "See that Captain Blackstar is comfortable," he ordered his steward. "Bring the miners and soldiers food and drink."

"Aye, Your Majesty," the steward said.

"And raise the grey pennant, so they know ashore that something's wrong."

"Aye, sir."

The passage home across the lake was heavy with woe. Galt looked back across the water to their landing spot and watched the fog roll onto the shore and creep across the lake. They were far beyond it now, but a different mist hung about every heart on board. It was heavy as a shroud.

Massie wept.

Tales of Old Natalia

Chapter Seven

Two weeks later, King Whitson came to Captain Blackstar's tent. He found Fleck sitting up and reading.

"I'm told you're much better, Captain," he said.

"I am, Your Majesty," Fleck said, leaving the bed to bow on one knee.

"How is your wound?"

"Much improved," Fleck said, rolling his arm slowly. "It's only a small injury."

"Come now, Blackstar. I'm no fool," Whitson said. "It was very near your heart. Doctor Grimes says you're fortunate to still be among us. She says that it's quite rare to survive a bowshot like that from such close range."

"I suppose I'm hard to kill," Fleck said, getting to his feet with a wince. "That may come in handy."

"It may indeed," Whitson said. "Thank you, Captain. Thank you for stepping in my place. Whatever it was that made that noise..." he trailed off, shaking his head.

"My place is beside you, my lord. Come what may."

"I hoped you would say that, because there's more work to do."

"I haven't been able to speak with my bucks, sir."

"That was by my order, Captain," the king said. "In consultation with Doctor Grimes, I decided to let you truly rest. But she assures me you are recovered enough to resume command."

"You don't mean to disband us, then?"

"No. I have something else in mind," he said, glancing to the corner, where Fleck's jacket, the one with the black star patch, hung. "Get dressed and follow me."

Fleck dressed quickly, pulling on his jacket at the last. His wound was tight, and it ached to extend his arm too much. But he was grateful to be allowed to leave, and so he said nothing. In a few moments, he followed the king outside. It was the first time he'd been allowed out since his injury. He had been told very little during his recovery and nothing about Gavin.

"Your bucks are working hard under Lieutenant Galt. But I'm afraid I have some bad news," the king said. He proceeded to tell him all that happened after he was shot and fell unconscious.

Fleck was furious. "Has nothing been done for the buck?" he asked. "I made him a promise."

"We have done far more than nothing," the king said. They crossed a walkway and moved through a field heavy with wheat toward the lakeshore. "As I said, your bucks are drilling daily with Galt, and they've been helping my crews with another project." They left the field and mounted a platform that overlooked the lake and the near shore. In the bay were three ships, *Vanguard* and two more.

"Three?" Fleck said, astonished. "Two more finished?"

"Almost," the king said, smiling. "In a few days we'll be ready to return to the far side of the lake and search for Gavin. We can also begin work on the mine. And I will explore the delta."

"But the uncanny sound we heard, my lord?" Fleck asked.

"I have been at it with my council for almost the entire time you've been recovering. I believe we need to return in force to see what is there. I want to own this lake. I want to be its master and find its farthest border. I want to know if there is actually passage west as I believe. I want to begin the mine and give you time to search for Gavin."

"May we go without you, Your Majesty?" Fleck asked. "It's very dangerous."

King Whitson shook his head and laughed. "There is no chance of that."

* * *

Fleck found his bucks helping on the third ship, Galt commanding and Burnley assisting him. They climbed down the ladders and gathered around him on the shore, each one delighted to see him well at last. They shook his hand, patted his back, and gave him short, nodding bows. "Welcome back," they said. "Have a good rest?" one asked. They laughed and fairly overwhelmed him with their rousing welcome.

58

"All right, all right," Galt called, "give the rabbit room to breathe. He's not back from the dead." But he didn't follow his own advice. He hooked an arm around his old friend, nearly dragging him into the water.

"I see you've been left in the charge of a mad-buck," Fleck said, shoving Galt away playfully. "You've done well," he said, looking at the ships. "They're even bigger than *Vanguard*."

"We mean to be ready, Fleck," Burnley said. "We don't mean to be caught off guard again."

"The large one will be the new flagship," Massie explained. "It's called *Lillie*."

"And the last?" Fleck asked.

"*Natalia*," Massie said. "Our way to a new world."

* * *

The week wore on, and the vigilance Fleck had always called for was now a matter of course for all the rabbits in the king's service. As he recovered his strength, he worked on the

MASSIE

59

boats, giving orders and drilling the bucks. In the early days of Black Star Company, before the fateful first voyage, Fleck had always ended each exercise by reciting the vow. When that time came on his first day back, the rabbits were reluctant, awkward. It was clear that Galt had not continued this rite during Fleck's absence.

As their drills ended, they began to break up and walk off.

"The vow!" Fleck shouted, and he drew his sword. They slowly reformed and raised their swords, Galt last of all.

"My place beside you! My blood for yours!" they called, though less enthusiastic than in the past.

"I know, bucks," Fleck said. "I know we all feel we let Gavin down."

"You saved him from killing the king," Massie said, his head down. "You haven't let us down. We've let you and Gavin down."

"I'm alive because of you, Massie," Fleck said, his hand absently finding his wound. "I'm alive because of you, Burnley. You, Kay Jack. And you, Lieutenant Galt." He looked at each of them as he spoke their names. Galt looked away. "I'm alive because you saved me, and you protected the king." He pointed across the water. "We go again, bucks. We go again."

Tales of Old Natalia

Chapter Eight

A t last the day of the return voyage came.
Fleck was up early, checking the mining inventory as it went aboard the three ships. Captain Grimble, a quiet, frosty rabbit, was overseeing the loading of *Vanguard*. He had been named its skipper. Captain Obbs, a happy, rotund rabbit of advancing age, did the same for *Natalia*. He had been given its command after serving as first lieutenant on the first journey. Lieutenant Walters was acting for King Whitson on *Lillie,* and *Lillie* carried most of their supplies. So Fleck worked the dock beside the flagship. He tugged on a barrel and handed it up to Burnley. A small, thin docker spoke to him.

"It's break time, ain't it?"

"I suppose we could take a short break," Fleck said, nodding to Burnley, who sat heavily on deck.

"Is you a lefty, Captain?" the docker asked. He dug in the pocket of his bright striped pants, which gathered at the knees. He fished out a pipe with his right hand and pointed its stem at his left. Like most sailors and dockers, he wore no shirt. He had an odd tangled rag wrapped around his head, with a hole for only one of his ears to stick out. This ear was bent halfway up so that it hung down and wobbled like a broken mast.

"I do favor my left," Fleck said, smiling. "But I'm able to use both."

"Folks say not to trust a lefty," the docker replied, plunging his pipe back into his pants. He cocked his head sideways and surveyed Fleck carefully. "But seein' as you use your right as well, I'll just business my own mind." He reached into his front pants pocket and once again fished out his pipe.

"Did you know the king is left-handed?" Fleck noticed the docker had very few teeth, but he chomped his empty unlit pipe with vigor, taking it out again to speak.

"Well o' course that's fine for royals, but you ain't a lord, is you?"

"Not by a long stretch. I'm a coal miner, like my father and his father and so on back."

"There ain't nothing minor about coal, son. We need it, and I'm glad your dad likes it. But don't he get dirty?" He replaced his pipe again, squinting one eye at Fleck and cocking his head even more sharply. His lone, bent ear caught in a sudden gust so that it stood straight up for a moment.

"Yes," Fleck said, trying not to smile as the ear fell again like a luffing sail. "It's hard work, and the coal dust fairly hangs in your fur."

"I dislike dust in the strongest terms," the docker said, waving his hand like a dust cloud had suddenly surrounded him. "Makes a feller sneeze, don't it?"

"It does," Fleck said.

"And since you brought up dust," the docker began, shaking his pipe at Fleck. He put it down and shook his head. "Never mind," he said, as if forgetting what he had been about to say. He stuffed the pipe back in his mouth and made to sit down on a barrel. But he hesitated and set about examining the barrel carefully, even laying his bent ear against it to listen for a moment. Then he sat.

"What is it?" Fleck asked.

"Only this," he said. "Did you ever hear a barrel whisper?"

"No."

"Me neither," he said, but he seemed uncertain.

Fleck laughed. "Been at it all night?"

"It weren't agin' the rules," he said. "I done it fair."

"Of course. But that makes for a long night. Are you all right?"

"Well, I used my left some," he said, lifting his pipe to his lips with his left hand, then quickly taking it out again with his right. "But I'm mostly right. But not in the head, if my Pap's ta' be believed."

"Your pap?"

"That's right, Lefty. My pap!" he said, shaking his head as if Fleck were the confused one. "My Pap said I had uncommon sense." He shoved the pipe back down into his pants pocket and crossed his left leg over his right. Then he switched and crossed his right over his left, fishing out his pipe again.

"That sounds good, actually. Uncommon sense?"

"Welp, it weren't meant that way, your honor," he said. Looking at his hand, he seemed to be surprised to find his pipe there, and he stuffed it back into his pocket with a frown. "He meant I didn't have none of what people calls common sense. Like lots of things, it sounds nicer-like than it means."

"I see."

"So do I," the docker said, fishing out his pipe again. He stuck it in his mouth, then swiftly yanked it out again, stuffing it into his pocket. "Me too, Lefty."

"What's your name, sir?"

"Now see here. I ain't a sir, and I been right-handed all my life. Folk calls me Jimmi Docker," he said, spitting on his right hand and

waving it to no one in particular. "Used to call me
Jimmi Smith, but I burnt my old master's forge
and was po-litely asked to find a 'nother profes-
sion. Then I was Jimmi Bricker, but my old master
dismissed me from that as well."

"You've had a lot of jobs, then?"

"Ah, twenty or so. The bricker weren't fair
with me. Wasn't him who I bricked into a room
with no doors; 'twas myself I did it to. Is that fair
they'd let a feller go for that? It weren't bad brick-
ing, neither. It took 'em four hours to break me
out, and all I had to eat was one single half-apple
what I kept in my pipe pocket."

"You've had an interesting life, it seems."

"I've give it a whirl," Jimmi said with a kick of
the barrel. He listened closely after the kick, like
he expected the barrel might protest, then nodded
and winked at Fleck.

Massie appeared, saluted Fleck, then climbed
aboard *Lillie*.

"What are you?" Jimmi asked, his face hint-
ing at betrayal. "I thought you wasn't a lord?
How's come Jack Quick there gave you the hand-
head wavy?"

"I'm captain of Black Star Company," Fleck

said. "We're hoping to found a coal mine across the water."

"Oh, a captain," Jimmi said, dragging out his pipe again. "But not a major one."

"No," Fleck said, smiling. "Quite the opposite. You *do* have uncommon sense, Jimmi Docker, and perhaps not all in the bad way."

"Believe what ya like," Jimmi said, then he stuffed the pipe between his teeth and grabbed onto the nearest barrel, hoisting it up to the waiting deckhands above. "My break's over, Minor Captain."

Fleck looked across the docks to where *Vanguard* was being loaded. He smiled to see the rabbits, dockers and sailors and many more, working cheerfully in a common cause. Then his eye fell on the command deck where Captain Grimble, his face bent in a menacing frown, whispered with his father, Lord Grimble.

Tales of Old Natalia

Chapter Nine

Fleck was arguing with the provisioner when the king, Queen Lillie, and Prince Lander came to the shore. The argument got quieter, and more civil. In fact, all across the docks and on board the ships, the loud shouts and constant chatter died down as the king approached and rabbits suddenly all looked sharp. That is, all except Jimmi Docker, who burst into an exuberant, unintelligible song. He was singing with his pipe in his mouth as he worked. Fleck shook his head as his argument with the provisioner continued in low tones.

The king had an argument of his own to deal with.

"I'm sorry, Lander," Whitson said. "You can't

come with us on this trip. I've told you, it's too dangerous."

"But I'm not afraid to fight beside you, Father," he said. "We aren't afraid, are we, Father?"

"You brave ones may not be," Queen Lillie said, "but I am afraid for you. You will stay here, son."

King Whitson nodded and bent to take his son's head in his hands. "Lander, I'm not sorry to tell you that I *am* afraid. I'm glad that I am. That tells me I need to be brave. I have been afraid so many times, my son. I will try to bring you out on the lake soon. For now, protect our home and obey your mother."

"Yes, sir," Prince Lander said, disappearing behind his mother's dress, tears in his eyes.

They said their goodbyes, and the three ships set out. All three had veteran crews, led by capable rabbits. Black Star Company joined the crew of *Lillie*.

"I see you have left your complement of rabbits at nine, Blackstar," King Whitson said, standing alongside the helm on

LANDER

72

the command deck. "I told you that you could take another buck to make ten."

"With respect, Your Majesty," Fleck said, touching his knuckle to his forehead as he bowed, "we already have ten."

"Of course," Whitson said. "I understand. I hope he's still alive as well. I pray we find what we long for this time."

"Whatever it was that made that screaming noise," Captain Vance said, "cannot possibly contend with so many soldiers."

"I hope you're right, Captain," Fleck said. "But I still say that vigilance is our clear duty. We can easily underestimate what we cannot easily understand."

"'Mysteries are only perils in disguise,'" King Whitson said, "or so said King Gerrard."

"Wisely," Fleck said.

"I expect good things," Captain Vance said. Fleck said nothing. He looked to the distant mountains with a steady gaze.

LILLIE

* * *

Captain Vance turned out to be right about this voyage. They made the far shore without incident, marched with a large band of soldiers to the dig site, and began their work. Captain Vance's soldiers guarded the perimeter in shifts while Fleck, Galt, and Burnley got the work underway around the site of Galt's discovery. It appeared to be a rich seam of coal. It wasn't long before they found a rhythm and all were occupied—the miners with their dig and the soldiers with their watch.

"We'll dig a bit more," Fleck told Captain Vance, "then we may lay our barrel of blastpowder and let it open up the site a bit."

"That will make quite a racket, will it not?" Vance asked.

"It will. Please go over this procedure with your soldiers, in case we do. When the blastpowder is laid ready, everyone is required to be at a safe distance, of course. But we still have protocols. When the fire is lit, the one who lights runs back, shouting, 'Burnout! Burnout!' If that shout is given, everyone must understand that it's time to flee and take cover."

"Understood, Captain Blackstar," Captain Vance said, and he walked off to relay this information to his lieutenants and soldiers. Fleck returned to the dig.

After an hour, Fleck and Massie finished a shift and were relieved by Galt and Kay Jack.

"I'm going for him," Fleck said to Galt.

"I don't think that's a good idea, Fleck," Galt answered.

"I know you don't," Fleck said. "Do what you do best and dig that coal, while I go hunt for Gavin."

"How many soldiers are you taking?"

"Just Massie," he said, and Massie came to his side, sword buckled on and bow slung over his back along with a quiver full of arrows.

"Fleck, really," Galt began, but Fleck cut him off.

"I leave the dig in your capable hands, Lieutenant Galt," he said. "Burnley will assist you, and Captain Vance is here as well. I'll return no later than an hour before sundown. If we aren't back then, please follow the plan and return to the ship. Assume we are staying on this side for the night."

"Fleck, don't do this—"

"Thank you, Lieutenant," Fleck said. He

motioned to Massie, nodded to Captain Vance, and hurried into the woods.

They passed the last sentinels in silence, Fleck cutting his way through tangled brush as Massie followed close behind. After an hour of walking, they reached a level wooded area, with thick moss and low limbs. Sunshine poured through the trees, illuminating a smooth dale beside a brook. Fleck halted and bent to refill his waterskin. Massie did the same.

"Did you hear anything?" Fleck asked, getting to his feet again.

"Nothing, sir. Not a single snap of the farthest, faintest twig."

"Nor I, Massie."

They walked on in silence, woe pooling around their hearts as if dammed.

Tales of Old Natalia

Chapter Ten

The sun was low when Fleck and Massie returned to camp, weary and dejected. There was no sign of Gavin.

"I'm sorry," Captain Vance said. "It always was a long shot. At least now you can move on."

Fleck said nothing. Frowning wearily, he crossed to the dig site and checked on the progress, getting a flat explanation from Galt.

"Burnley," Fleck said, "please oversee the dig for another hour and then settle the camp for the night. Lieutenant Galt and Captain Vance will accompany me to meet the king on the shore. We'll most likely sail with him to Seddleton tonight and return in the morning with fresh supplies. Remember your training," he said, looking over his company. He glanced out at the thick forest, and his face fell. He whispered, "And take care of one another." Massie sat beneath a tree with his head down. No one bothered him.

Captain Vance nodded to his own lieutenant, Joyner, to follow him as another took charge of the soldiers left on site. Ten more soldiers followed the captains and their first lieutenants back toward the shore.

"Will the king come to the camp?" Joyner asked.

"I hope not," Captain Vance said. "He may well opt to resupply since we have an established site in the works."

"It's good we'll have coal," Galt said, looking at Fleck.

Fleck nodded, his mouth a tight, thin slit.

In a little while they made the shore and found soldiers guarding the beach. King Whitson received them on his flagship's command deck with a meal. They ate and drank together as *Lillie,* with *Natalia* at her side, carried them home.

"I'm very sorry the search failed," King Whitson said as Fleck picked at his food. "But it's awfully good news that the mine appears to be operational. It will do so much for our comfort and safety. And it will help calm a few political squalls. Congratulations are in order." He raised his glass and saluted Fleck.

Fleck nodded. He said, "Thank you for believing in this mission, Your Majesty." But he sounded exhausted and deeply sad.

"Blackstar," King Whitson said, "I know it's not easy to lose rabbits. I do. As you well know, we've lost many on this journey. I have felt every loss keenly, as though I lost a part of my own soul. It will never grow easy, but it's necessary to know when to move on."

"I understand, sir," Fleck said. "I will attend to the mine."

"I am ever so sorry, Captain."

Fleck nodded thanks and looked away, wiping his eyes.

Lillie rose and fell in a gentle rhythm as they finished their meal. They drank to the king and to the new world they hoped to create in Natalia. The blue sky deepened to purple, then black. Stars appeared, and night fell.

After supper, Fleck wandered the ship, staring into the darkness toward the high, bleak

mountains beyond their fledgling mine. The ship's hands gave him a wide berth. He could see thin slivers of orange light through the woods in the foothills. *Soon,* he thought, *those fires will spread to Seddleton and fuel its boundless progress.* It ought to have made him happy, but the echoing memory of those terrible screeches made him restless, and Gavin's loss filled his heart with woe.

"Blackstar," King Whitson said, approaching with slow consideration. "May I join you?" Fleck bowed, and the king came to stand beside him. Fleck noticed the king was wearing his crown, something he rarely did. It was a lovely crown, and it glowed golden in the moonlight. The peaks were tips of forged fire, and the embers along the base were all of orange and red. It was a crown of frozen flames, glorious and beautiful. Fleck had never seen it this close.

They stood silently as the breeze carried *Lillie* along at a leisurely pace. They stared into the lake and past it, to the fading lights of the camp and the mountains beyond. King Whitson finally spoke. "What will you name it?"

"The mine, Your Majesty?"

"Yes."

"I'd like to be sure it's secure before naming it, sir. It feels unlucky to name it just yet. Like we'd be inviting trouble."

"There's such a thing as too much caution," Whitson said.

Fleck sighed.

The king went on. "Let's look at it another way. If you had a small mining settlement, one that became a town, what would you name it?"

"It's not for me to name, sir. I'd be happy to call it whatever you like," Fleck said.

"I'd like it if you named it."

"Perhaps after my father, then?"

"Jonston?" King Whitson said. "It's a good name."

"Perhaps," Fleck said. His sadness only grew.

"It's a deep thing, fathers and sons," Whitson said, tossing a thick splinter into the lake.

"It is."

King Whitson looked back at Seddleton, then at Fleck. "I want to tell you something, Captain. Something few others know."

"Yes, sir?"

"As you know," King Whitson began, "my father perished in the last stand on Golden Coast, fighting beside the old king—the same hallowed place your own father fell as a hero."

Fleck nodded, looking out over the water again.

"You know the king had no heir and that he appointed me to lead our people. In his last council with me, he gave me the Ruling Stone." He fished in his shirt and brought out the dazzling ruby attached to a gold chain. "He also gave me a trunk filled with many other treasures. It included this crown, which, for some time, kings only wore on very special occasions. Other things he gave me, holy things." The king looked from side to side. His voice dropped to a hoarse whisper. "Did you ever wonder what happened to the Stone Book of Fay and to Flint's sword?" He shook his head and went on. "But I haven't come to speak of those things. I came to tell you of the crown. The king told me of the crown's origin, of an old tradition he had hoped to reintroduce but was unable to when his only son died. The tradition was the selection of the heir and bestowment of the Green Ember."

Fleck straightened, studying the king's eyes and the crown above them. Both were alive with light. The king went on.

"The Green Ember is the large center stone of this crown," he said, pointing to an empty indention in the crown's wrought gold. "Well, it's usually there. In the old tradition, a king made succession clear by passing the emerald to his heir. The prince kept it as a down payment of his future inheritance and a sacred stewardship to guard while he awaited the day of his own rule. So, if the crown of flames falls . . ." King Whitson paused, scanning the lights of Seddleton.

"The Green Ember rises," Fleck finished.

"Yes," King Whitson said. "You understand me. I am afraid to speak too openly of these things, but I need my best rabbits to know in case the worst ever happens. I need my captains to be sure of their duty."

Fleck knelt slowly, his eyes on the king. He touched the king's feet tenderly. "My lord, I would be honored to trade my life for yours. I would gladly die to preserve the queen's life or Prince Lander's. I will be loyal to the end."

Tales of Old Natalia

Chapter Eleven

Dawn broke. After a fitful night's sleep ashore, Fleck made his way to the docks. He saw Jimmi Docker, along with several others, as they loaded the last of the supplies onto *Lillie* and *Natalia*. Jimmi noticed him and came shuffling over.

"Mornin', Cap'n Lefty," Jimmi said, touching his unlit pipe to his forehead in salute.

"Good morning, Jimmi. How's the loading been?"

"All completely good, except for the bad parts," he said, plunging his pipe into his pants pocket.

"What do you mean?"

"Well, there was the small matter of a fire—"

"A fire?" Fleck said, his eyes growing wide.

"The blastpowder!"

"It weren't aboard ships, your honor," Jimmi said, putting up his hands. "It were over in them trees. A very small fire indeed."

Fleck sighed. "I'm awake now," he said, shaking his head. "You scared me half to death."

"Beg your pardon, Cap," Jimmi said, looking into his empty hand as if it were missing something. He looked up, disappointed. "This was dark and early, and there was just a few of us here. We all went over and put it out quick-like."

"Good," Fleck said. "I think I'll have a look."

"Have a peek, if you like. It's just some leaves burnt and a bit of paper."

Fleck did investigate, but he found it just as Jimmi had said.

"The barrels haven't been whispering to you again, have they?" Fleck asked, walking back onto the dock beside *Lillie*.

"I think they must have caught cold," Jimmi said, taking his pipe out of his mouth and smiling wide. "I heard one sneeze."

"We shall have to send Doctor Grimes down immediately," Fleck said, smiling. "We need healthy barrels." He nodded to Jimmi and boarded

Lillie. Galt was there, leaning against the rail.

"Sleep okay?" Galt asked. Fleck shook his head. "Me either," Galt said, blocking a yawn with his hand.

"We have work," Fleck said, nodding to *Natalia*. Galt seemed almost ready to say something, but after a moment's hesitation he nodded and moved toward the dock as Fleck went below.

* * *

Fleck checked *Lillie's* cargo against his manifest. Both *Lillie* and *Natalia* had been resupplied during the night, and he wanted to be sure they had all they would need that day. Jimmi and the other dockers were hard workers, but Fleck felt the need to double-check them. He noted thirty-seven barrels of blastpowder, twenty-five pickaxes and as many shovels, eight wheelbarrows, and several casks of water, ale, foodstuffs, and other equipment. He noted the nails and other supplies necessary for building permanent structures at the camp. *This is really happening. If not for losing Gavin, I would be very happy.* He had seen all this material on shore the night before, so he didn't examine everything closely. He was due to meet the king.

S. D. Smith

Galt returned and handed him the approved manifest from *Natalia's* hold. Fleck nodded and handed him the one he had worked on.

"I'm supposed to meet the king," he said.

"I'll finish this up," Galt said.

Fleck almost said something to thaw the cold relationship between himself and Galt. But he didn't. Galt nodded and went to work while Fleck climbed the ladder and went above deck.

"Good morning, Blackstar," King Whitson said as Fleck emerged. "It's a lovely day to sail, is it not?"

"Aren't they all?" Fleck said, a small smile appearing.

"Indeed," Whitson said. "But this wind! Marvelous. Clear away, and raise anchor!" he called. "Make all sail. Let's get back to our bucks across the water."

The crew went to work and the sails were raised, catching the wind as the ship made way.

Fleck was not as taken with sailing as was the king, but when the sails rose and filled, his heart rose with them. He smiled as the ship was carried along at an increasing clip, the wake making a wide white V behind them. Glancing across at

Natalia, he smiled and saluted Captain Obbs, who was eating a pasty and sipping a large mug of coffee. Seeing *Natalia's* sails full and majestic, he worried briefly about what would happen if the wind died, but he cast this thought aside.

They raced past Dobble's Point and were well on their way when Fleck spoke. "I see your family did not come to the dock this time. I hope Her Majesty and His Royal Highness are well."

"They *are* well, thank you," the king said. "Last night I broke the news to Prince Lander that he was not to accompany us on our return trip, and he was—how shall I say it—Most displeased."

Fleck smiled. "His Royal Highness has spirit. It will serve him well when he is king."

"But he must learn obedience," the king said. "That will serve him better."

Fleck nodded, then scanned the far shoreline, looking for signs of activity. He could see nothing to alarm him. Still, when he looked beyond the shore to the foothills and the high, bleak mountains beyond, he shuddered and looked away.

Soon Galt appeared on deck, a worried look on his face. *Were the counts off?* He walked swiftly toward the command deck where Fleck and King

Whitson stood. "Your Majesty," he said. "May I show you something below deck?"

"Certainly, Lieutenant," King Whitson said, "but you should address your captain first."

"Yes, sir," he said. "Captain Blackstar, you will want to see this as well."

Fleck frowned but followed Galt to the hatch and down the ladder to the hold. The king instructed Lieutenant Walters to take command, then followed Fleck and Galt below.

Fleck reached the bottom of the ladder and turned. There, sitting on a crate, was Prince Lander. The prince wore a grey shirt and a worried expression. A gold chain dangled a bright emerald from his neck.

"Lander!" King Whitson said. "What have you done?"

"I snucked out this morning and hid in a barrel," the young rabbit said. He sniffed and rubbed his nose. "I want to sail with you, Father."

"I want you to sail with me, too, Lander," Whitson said, "but at the right time. This was not only disobedience to me, son, but you have also let our subjects down. You have caused them extra work and worry. It is selfish and unkind."

Lander nodded, his head dropping low.

"Being a ruler is, contrary to popular notions, a calling of self-sacrifice. That is, if one wants to be a good ruler.

"My son, my dear young buck," Whitson continued, coming close and looking into Lander's eyes, "we are not of Gan and Shambler. We are heirs of Flint and Fay. That is your story, son."

Fleck and Galt had retreated to the hatchway ladder and were trying to disappear quietly. But King Whitson motioned them forward.

"Son, you owe these good rabbits an apology," King Whitson said.

Prince Lander squirmed, looked around, and finally met his father's gaze. "Yes, Father."

He slid off the crate and walked slowly to Fleck, kneeling before him. Fleck looked at King Whitson, his eyes protesting the prince's actions. But the king shook his head. He would have to endure it.

"I'm so sorry, Captain Blackstar," Prince Lander said. "And Lieutenant Galt, I beg you for your forgiveness. What I did was selfish, and I won't do it again, not ever never. I will do much better in the future, sirs."

"Of course we forgive Your Royal Highness,"

Fleck said, unable to keep from taking the prince's hand and helping him up. "We were young rabbits once as well, eager to be with our fathers and to do the same work they did. We understand."

King Whitson put his arm around Lander, moving his hand to tuck the dangling emerald beneath the prince's shirt. He thanked Fleck and Galt and dismissed them, then turned to speak further with his son. As  Fleck ascended the ladder, he heard tender words from King Whitson.

On deck again, Galt said quietly to Fleck, "I like that lad."

"Me too," Fleck said. "He will be a fine king."

"And we will be miners again," Galt said, reaching to shake hands with Fleck. Fleck smiled and shook Galt's hand.

"My place beside you," he said. Then, looking at the shore, "Let's build the best mine in all of Natalia."

Chapter Twelve

They reached the shore without incident, Prince Lander now on deck with his father. As the anchor fell, they called across to Captain Grimble of *Vanguard*. Grimble, always spare with his words, reported that it had been a quiet night.

"Captains Blackstar and Vance," King Whitson said, "please visit the camp and, if you find all is well, send rabbits back for the supplies."

"Yes, Your Majesty."

"With Your Majesty's permission," Captain Vance said, "I will also exchange some rabbits who have been at the camp with those on board the ship."

"As you think best, Captain Vance."

Captain Vance, Joyner, Fleck, and Galt

95

bowed, then clambered down the rope ladders. Wading into the water, they made their way to the shore, where several soldiers had established a small camp. A charcoal fire burned low, and the bucks all looked tired. The sleepy-eyed soldiers repeated the same report they had heard from *Vanguard's* skipper. A quiet night. Nothing to report. But Fleck noticed that one of them was looking away.

"What about you, soldier?" Fleck asked. "Was it a quiet night, as they say?"

The soldier looked from Captain Blackstar to the forest, then at Captain Vance.

"Answer him, Shel," Captain Vance said.

"I don't like to contradict anyone," he said, eyeing the lieutenant who had given the report. "It's only that I, well..." he stuttered and finally was silent.

"Let's have it," Fleck said. "No matter how insignificant it seems to you, we need to know."

"We...Captain," he said. "I never heard nothing particular through the watch, just normal forest sounds that make your mind wonder, but I felt like," he shook his head, "it felt like we were being watched all night."

"Did some of you other bucks feel the same?" Captain Vance asked. Several others nodded nervously, glancing at the lieutenant in charge.

Fleck frowned at Galt as Captain Vance had a quiet word with his lieutenant.

"It might be nothing," Galt said. "It's easy to get spooked out here."

Fleck nodded, his eyes taking in the surrounding coast and the thick forest ahead.

* * *

After a few more minutes, they left the shoreline and made their way into the forest. The path was getting clearer now, and they knew their way. In a short time they reached the camp. Soldiers came to attention as Vance and Joyner asked for reports. Burnley emerged from what was now a deep shaft and greeted Fleck and Galt.

"You have made so much progress," Fleck said. "Well done!"

"Thanks, Fleck," Burnley said, smiling. "I won't lie. We've done well. The shaft is already quite deep, and we've prepped several spots for blastpowder. We'll blow open a seam so rich we'll have coal enough for a hundred winters."

"It's rich, then?" Galt asked, slapping Fleck's back.

"It is," Burnley said. The rest of Black Star Company gathered around, and Fleck saw that even Massie was smiling again.

"Well done, bucks!" Fleck shouted. "The king will be delighted to hear it. Burnley, you and Massie shall report to the king in my name, and Galt and I will join in the work. A bit of digging will do us good."

"I'm for that," Galt said, laying aside his jacket. "You'll need ten rabbits from among the soldiers and the rested to carry back supplies."

"Understood," Burnley said. "And I'm plenty honored, Fleck, that you'd let me give our news to the king."

"And the prince," Galt said.

"The prince too? Oh my. Not the queen, I hope?" Burnley said, swabbing his dirty face with his equally filthy handkerchief. "I don't think I'd be likely enough to survive that."

"No," Fleck said, smiling. "Queen Lillie is not on board. It's only the king and Prince Lander."

"Oh, only King Whitson Mariner, who saved us all, and Prince Lander, the heir to the throne?

S. D. Smith

Sure enough, lads. Never worry for me!"

"Relax, old friend," Fleck said, slapping Burn-ley's shoulder. "You know the king, and the prince is, well—he's feeling humble today."

"Let's go, Burnley," Massie said. "I'm ready to stretch my legs in the sunshine."

As Fleck reached the mouth of the cave, a loud whining echoed down the mountain.

"Not again," Galt said, reaching for his sword.

Tales of Old Natalia

Chapter Thirteen

The soldiers drew their swords, and Captain Vance ordered his bucks to form a hasty perimeter. The dirty bucks of Black Star Company filled in the gaps.

"Steady," Fleck called, walking slowly toward the noise. Fingering the hilt of his sword, he scanned the trees. There was no fog this time, but everything else felt eerily familiar. His wound, which he had hardly thought of for days, began to throb.

The whine sounded again, and the bowmen scanned the forest. Whatever it was, it was close. Fleck frowned, his eyebrows creased. He waved his arm quickly, demanding silence.

The whine came again, this time more distant.

It sounded wild, mad, but it trailed off on the wind.

Fleck's eyes grew wide, and, without a backward glance, he bolted into the forest.

"Captain?" Vance shouted. "Captain Blackstar!"

Massie was the first to break after him. Then the whole company of miners was splitting the woods on the heels of their leader. Galt came last.

"Hold here!" Captain Vance shouted as some of his soldiers made to follow. "Hold!"

Fleck dodged through heavy brush, branches snapping as he laid into them with wild sword strokes.

Massie caught up to him and silently moved through the dense forest beside his captain. Up the mountain they climbed, through damp and heavy trees and moss-covered ground. After a short time, Fleck stopped, calling back for the trailing bucks to be quiet. He waited, heard nothing, then resumed his wild scramble, Massie tearing in behind him.

The sound came again, a shrieking whine of hysterical despair. Fleck turned toward the sound and surged through the forest, leaping fallen limbs and slicing through briars and brambles. They heard rushing water and broke into a clearing on the edge of a high waterfall, the stream below winding down toward the lake.

There on the cliff's edge sat Gavin.

He was thin, and his eyes were wild. Patches of bare skin broke the pattern of mottled fur that had once covered his body. He was shivering, mumbling to himself, and pulling on his ears.

"Coming, coming, coming, coming, coming, coming, coming, coming," he mumbled. "Terrors, terrors, terrors, terrors, coming, coming, coming..." He went on and on. Fleck signaled for Massie to creep back and silence the mad crashing of the bucks who followed behind. Massie nodded, then disappeared into the trees.

Fleck crept slowly toward Gavin, his hands extended in a gesture of calm assurance. "I'm coming to sit beside you, Gavin," he said. "I'm your friend. Remember me? I'm Fleck."

"Terrors!" Gavin shouted, scooting closer to the precipice. "Coming! Terrors!" He resumed the shrieking whine that so reminded Fleck of the noise they'd heard that first day at the mine site. *Had there been another lost rabbit in the woods?*

No, it was different somehow. "Terrors and flames, ruin and rage, hatred from on high!" Gavin shouted. "Coming, coming, coming, coming, coming, coming, coming, coming, coming, coming, coming, coming, coming!"

Fleck saw that Massie, Kay Jack, and Brephen were standing at the edge of the forest, waiting for instructions.

"I'm going to sit beside you, Gavin," Fleck said in a calm voice. "And you can tell me all about it."

"Noooooooo!" Gavin shrieked, turning toward Fleck for the first time. His wild eyes terrified Fleck, and his ranting continued, broken only by the high-pitched wailing screech he chanted again and again. "Terrors, terrors, terrors! Coming, coming, coming, coming!"

Fleck was near enough to touch him now. Gavin's screeches trailed off into incessant mumbled repetitions of "terror" and "coming." Fleck reached out to touch Gavin's shoulder. When he did, Gavin turned, and for a brief moment Fleck saw recognition in the young rabbit's eyes.

"Captain?" In his voice there was surprise and, for the briefest moment, relief. He spoke in a flat tone. "Captain. It's the end of the world." Then the terror returned and spiraled out in mad shrieks and screams. "Coming! Coming, coming, coming . . ."

"Help me!" Fleck shouted. He grabbed Gavin and rolled him away from the cliff's edge. Massie and the others rushed in. After a struggle, they managed to restrain him, making him as comfortable as possible. They carried him back down the mountain to camp.

"Coming," he mumbled all the way. "Terror. Coming, coming, coming . . ."

* * *

They neared the camp, calling out as they approached to let their fellows know who they were.

"What's this?" Captain Vance asked as they entered the camp bearing the frail, mumbling rabbit with tattered clothes and mad eyes. "Is it him?"

"It's our Gavin," Massie said, stroking Gavin's head and whispering gently to him. "It's all right, my friend. We'll take care of you, and we'll bring you home safe."

"Safe?" Gavin said, speaking clearly for a moment. "We are *not* safe!"

"Quiet, everyone," Fleck said, silencing the uproar in the camp. "It's all right, Gavin," he said, motioning for calm. He nodded to Massie.

"Why aren't we safe, Gavin?" Massie asked.

"Terror, terror, terror," he began.

"I know, I know," Fleck said gently. "I know you're scared. But you're back with your company now. I'm here with you. Massie's here. And we'll see that you're taken care of. We'll protect you, Gavin, just as we promised. My place beside you, my blood for—"

"There will be blood, Captain," Gavin said; then he resumed his chant. "Coming, coming, coming, coming, coming, coming—"

"Who is coming?" Fleck interrupted, his eyes darting to the tree line and up to the peaks beyond. "Who is coming?"

Gavin's eyes, which had been alive with madness, went out like a torch dropped in water. He looked to the mountains, pointed high up, and said quietly, "The monsters, Captain. The monsters."

Chapter Fourteen

Gavin faded, clinging lightly to life. He would say no more, and he drifted into a kind of sleep from which no one could rouse him for a long time. Massie stayed by his side and cared for him while the captains met with their lieutenants.

"What do we make of this?" Vance asked. Joyner stood alongside Captain Vance, while Galt and Fleck stood opposite, and Fleck kept an uneasy eye on Massie and Gavin.

"Begging your pardon, Captain Blackstar," Joyner said, "but Gavin's mad. We need to get him back to Seddleton and carry on the work. I don't want to abandon the mine just because of the ravings of a starving rabbit."

"I agree," Galt said, looking at Fleck. Fleck's

eyes continued to move from Gavin to the mountain peaks, as if he was searching for the connection.

"We need to get Gavin back, I agree," Fleck said. "He needs more help than we can give him on this side. But I fear there may be something in his warning. Remember the wild, uncanny sound we heard. What if Gavin's right?"

"Then there are monsters here," Joyner said, smiling. But the others didn't smile.

"It may be exactly as Gavin has described it," Fleck said.

"But Fleck, what if it's nothing?" Galt asked.

"Then we lose a little time on the mine," Fleck said. "What if it's something?"

"Then we have to protect the king," Captain Vance said. "And the prince," he added.

The prince! The Green Ember. How could I have forgotten? "Yes," Fleck said. "We must be extra cautious in light of the prince's presence."

"Agreed," Vance said, "but we should not be so hasty that we—"

The uncanny sound returned, a screeching horror multiplied tenfold in the echoing valley between the foothills of the mountains. Fleck wondered how he could have ever mistaken Gavin's mad whine for this terrifying shriek. He looked to the heights and saw black shapes leaping from the mountains in the distance.

The monsters were coming.

* * *

The rabbits panicked, tripping over their gear in a desperate flight.

"Hold your position, bucks!" Fleck shouted. Black Star Company formed around him.

Captain Vance was screaming at his soldiers, but many had already dashed toward the path to shore.

"We have to move, Fleck!" Galt called, panic in his eyes.

"We will!" Fleck shouted, signaling with his hand toward the shore. "Together now, and get your weapons!"

Chaos threatened to engulf the rabbits, but their captains

BURNLEY

fought against it, leading their bucks toward the shore in something like an orderly manner. Burnley took the frail form of Gavin on his back, and Massie followed behind with his bow at the ready. Galt went in front, shouting back for them all to move faster. Fleck took up the rear and covered the flight alongside Captain Vance.

They stormed through clusters of trees, making better time than ever along their new-made path back to shore. Still, it felt painfully long. When they came to a break in the trees, Fleck whirled and looked toward the heights of the distant mountains. The sight filled him with terror. Flying monsters leapt from the heights of distant peaks and beat their black wings, filling the sky. They were advancing toward the lake. Toward the king. They seemed to have flames for feet and blades for faces. The speed of their approach was terrible. Fleck stumbled, then charged on, unable for a moment even to shout for his company to hurry. He glanced at Captain Vance. His stunned expression told Fleck they had both seen the same thing.

At last they broke through the trees that hid the shore. They found a chaotic scene on the beach. *Vanguard*, in a panic, had already set sail for Seddleton. *Lillie* remained at anchor alongside *Natalia*. The remaining ships couldn't hold all the rabbits, so they were trying to signal *Vanguard* to return.

"Captain, what is this?" King Whitson shouted when Fleck finally found him. They were on the shore, surrounded by wild splashing, harried shouts, and the general din of panic. Worst of all, the distant haunting screeches could be heard over everything. Whitson had one hand on his sword, and the other clung tightly to Prince Lander's small hand.

"Gavin called them monsters, Your Majesty," Fleck called above the racket.

The piercing screeches rebounded off the lake and filled the air. Rabbits across the shoreline and on board the ships cowered, trembling at the sound. Some dove to the ground. Fleck crouched, then stood again, spinning to survey the sky.

It was an unspeakable terror. Hordes of massive flying creatures filled the distant sky. Less distant every moment.

"Sir," he shouted to the king, "I think we could keep you safer at the mine!"

"No, sir! The ships!" Captain Vance shouted. "That's where all the soldiers are." Only a few soldiers remained on shore, bravely surrounding the king's conference.

"It's too open!" Fleck shouted. By now the Black Star miners had gotten Gavin on board *Lillie,* and most stood nearby to help cover the king and await Fleck's orders.

"We have a stiff breeze. It backed an hour ago, and it's heading the right way," King Whitson shouted, eyeing the sky, the distant shore, and the set of the ships. "We've fought at sea before, captains. I'd rather trust to what we know. The water."

The king had no sooner spoken than Fleck sprang into action.

"To the ships!" he shouted, motioning for his bucks to follow the king onboard *Lillie.* "Double time and bows at the ready. Protect the king and prince!"

They splashed through the shallow water, then waded in to reach the rope ladders. Once on board, they spun to survey the approaching threat. The deck was full, too full. *Vanguard* had not taken enough rabbits on board to evenly distribute the crews. *Lillie's* hands shouted for the soldiers and miners to move while they made the vessel ready to sail. Agonizing seconds passed before they got moving. But the breeze was strong, and at last they were underway.

"Hoist the grey pennant!" King Whitson shouted, still holding Lander's hand.

Fleck stood by the king, breathing hard. He scanned the sky, from the forest behind to Seddleton ahead, his mind full of woeful estimations. As if he was reading Fleck's mind, the king shook his head.

"We cannot beat them to shore. It's not possible." Fleck knew it to be true.

"Still," the king said aloud, glancing at Prince Lander, "we'll get as close as we can."

"Yes, sir."

"All hands, move portside and hug the rails!" King Whitson shouted. Fleck made to move. "Not you, Captain. Stay by my side. I need to steer with both hands." The king looked at the small furry hand that so tightly held his own, then lifted it and placed the young prince's hand in Fleck's. Fleck's big grey hand closed on it, and he bent to look the prince in the eye as King Whitson took the wheel from his first lieutenant.

"I'm going to stay with you, Your Royal Highness," Fleck said, "until your father can be with you again, or until the end of this."

"Is it the end of the world?" Prince Lander asked.

"I don't know. But even if it is, I'll stand beside you."

"What if you have to steer?" Prince Lander asked, trembling.

"I'm an expert at one-handed steering," Fleck said. "And I've never lost a buck in my company."

"Never?"

"Never," Fleck said, glancing at Massie and Gavin. "Would you like to be in Black Star Company?"

"Yes!" Prince Lander said. "Do I get a star patch?"

"Of course you do. I'll have one for you as soon as I can."

"I can be brave," Prince Lander said.

"Good. You must be brave to be a miner or a soldier," Fleck said. "It's the rules."

The prince nodded. He understood about rules.

For a few moments Fleck ignored the

surrounding tumult and focused his gaze on Prince Lander's face. The terrors faded for a moment, and Fleck saw in the little prince's eyes a new world awaiting. He saw rabbits thriving in a safe place, under the steady leadership of Lander, a king now, strong and wise. The picture came to him in a rush, all at once, and he loved it.

It was the little prince who spoke, arresting Fleck's waking dream. "You don't seem afraid, Captain Blackstar," he said. "You're smiling." Fleck realized that he was and that now the prince was smiling too.

"I *am* afraid," Fleck said, tenderly touching the prince's head. "But I keep on loving what's on the other side of this fight. And that will have to make me brave."

"There!" King Whitson called. "They come." Fleck spun and saw them.

Monsters.

Tales of Old Natalia

Chapter Fifteen

They swooped down in a wave over the mine site, the tree line, and the water's edge. As the monsters came closer, they dropped low over the water. They looked like a wave of black fog dotted with bright orange rolling up to meet the ships. Fleck turned Prince Lander away from the scene. He glanced back, however, trying to locate his bucks. He looked at Massie, who was finally getting Gavin to eat and drink a very little, and at Kay Jack, Brephen, Hollis, and the rest, who checked their weapons and shook their heads. They all stood portside along with most of the crew and soldiers, but there was Galt, standing on the prow of the ship like a statue. Like the rest, he was stunned into silence.

King Whitson shouted, "Stay on the port side as long as you can. When they attack, be bold. Remember the heroes of Golden Coast and do your worst!"

A shout rang out, a cry to aid their wavering belief. Fleck took an offered spyglass from King Whitson. The black wave of monsters approached, wings beating in time. Through the glass, Fleck could see their sharp, pointed beaks. Their feet were long and fitted with vicious blades. Many wore black armor and most bore torches.

"These are the birds of prey," Whitson said. "I fear legends have become real and our nightmares chase us into daytime."

"Legends or no, they are creatures and can be killed," Fleck said.

"Let us hope so." Whitson's steward fastened the straps of his breastplate as the king gripped the helm. He held tight, and wind filled the sails, driving them on.

"The wind is for us, Your Majesty," Fleck said. Was it possible to make it across before the monsters were on them?

"If it stays like this," Whitson began, but he

118

did not go on. They both looked from the sky to the town and back, silently urging the wind to blow like it had never blown before.

Lieutenant Walters returned to the command deck. "Your Majesty, if we carry on like this we'll need to reduce sail. The strain is telling, and the foremast is cracking."

"Thank you, Lieutenant," he said. "We will carry on."

"She'll come down, sir!"

"If we take in sail, Walters, we'll be torn apart," the king said, nodding to the sky behind them. "Make the foremast fast by binding it with rope as well as ever you can. It won't hold together long but may buy us a little time."

"Yes, sir," Lieutenant Walters said. He ran off, barking commands to several hands. In a moment, they were charging past, bearing great coils of rope. These they uncoiled, wrapped around the fractured foremast, and tightened carefully. Wrap and tighten, wrap and tighten, on and on they worked. Soon Walters reported to the king.

"The foremast is as secure as we may make her, sir," he said.

"Thank you, Lieutenant," the king said. "Please ask Captain Vance to come to me at his earliest convenience."

Walters nodded, then turning, he shouted, "Pass the word for Captain Vance."

Fleck marveled again at the calm courtesy displayed by the king and his hands, even amid a terrifying chase.

Soon Captain Vance appeared. "Your Majesty?"

"Captain, please be sure that every archer we have is on deck, every available arrow at hand."

"Very good, sir." Vance turned and called for Joyner, and together they saw all the archers armed.

"If we, by some miracle, make land before…" Fleck looked back at the steady approach of their pursuers. "What, then, are your orders?"

"We do whatever we can, Blackstar," King Whitson said. "It will be an awful fight. But we must get as many as possible to safety." Here he glanced at Prince Lander. "We must think about the future."

"I understand, sir," Fleck said. The wind blew hard, and he turned to survey the sky. Of course the wind carried the birds on faster as well, but the ships seemed to outpace them. A slow hope grew in Fleck. The hands sensed it as well. The mood on board was shifting.

Lieutenant Walters approached, a smile on his face. "It seems we'll make it to shore before them after all, sir. As long as the wind holds."

Even as he spoke, the wind slowed and all but died. The ships coasted on, but now the black wave of terror surged, gaining on the ships with awful ease. Fleck moved to the rail and gazed at Seddleton. It was still too far to swim to shore, at least for most of the rabbits. They were near the harbor, and Dobble's Point loomed on their right, but it would do little good to make land there. They would be farther still from Seddleton, and they would be easy targets for the birds.

King Whitson looked at Fleck and shook his head. He smiled quickly at Lander, then called above the noise. "Be brave, bucks. Sell your lives dearly and slow their advance. We all have loved ones, little ones and sweethearts, back home. Every moment we delay the enemy counts. Use the boathooks. Run ropes through the rigging like a web. Make it hard on these devils. Do all you can and be brave!"

Fleck raised a shout along with the rest. The king was right. The only possible goal was to slow the advance, to distract their attackers and buy time for those ashore to get to safety. He expected none on board the three ships to survive.

"Archers!" Whitson called out. "Prepare a volley on my mark." Standing along the rails, they nocked their arrows and waited.

"Black Stars!" Fleck called. "Bows at the ready!" Those who could obeyed and joined their fellows at the railing. Fleck saw Massie draw his bow, with three arrows nocked and a wild fury in his eyes. Just behind him knelt Gavin, like Massie's own ghost. Though he had eaten and drunk during the voyage across, for now he could only watch.

As the archers stood ready, the bravest hands went aloft, spreading rope through the rigging as the king had commanded.

Hideous screeches filled the air. Rabbits flinched and fell, some from the tops, to crash on deck. The beating of the birds' wings came to the rabbits like the bellows of death. They screeched and shrieked, and the eerie whine came over the water like brittle doom broken and shattering on the ships. Terror came before them, and only the bravest could continue the preparations the king had ordered.

Then they were there. The monsters were above them.

Tales of Old Natalia

Chapter Sixteen

Archers, let fly!" King Whitson shouted. And they did. From *Lillie* and *Natalia*, the arrows flew up. The birds banked at the last moment, and most of the hail missed. Yet some found their mark, and a few satisfying splashes followed as some of the foremost monsters spun into the water. But many others came. Arrows whizzed between them and glanced off their armor. In their feet they bore torches and little flaming pots.

The enemy descended, swooping overhead, dropping their fiery burdens on the ships. These burst in small explosions and spread. All three ships were fighting fires at once. But the mass of the dark force flew ahead, past the ships, toward Seddleton.

Fleck watched in horror. In a few panicked moments, fire rained down on Seddleton.

"There are at least a hundred of them," Whitson said, taking charge of Lander again. "And their fire catches and grows, so they have some evil art with it."

The black force banked over Seddleton, and most flew back with great speed toward the ships. Others dropped deftly in and tore through the town. Terrified cries and a noise of destruction came to them over the water.

"Vile monsters!" Fleck shouted. "Come to us!"

They could not have heard him, but they did come, and in tremendous numbers. Nearly all the rabbits fled the tops, and many made for the hatchways and dove below deck. Most of those remaining were huddled on the deck, looking for some small place of refuge. The monsters beat their wings and raced toward *Lillie.* Against every instinct, Fleck began to climb the rigging.

The noise of their wings grew as strong as a storm. Fleck reached the foremast yard top, just below the red-diamond standard of King Whitson Mariner. He drew his sword. The leaders headed straight for him, screeching as they came and extending their horrible talons.

He didn't wait for them to find him. He drew his sword and leapt. Swinging wildly, he met the enemy aloft. His strokes, all but one, met air. The one found a black breastplate. Its owner clawed at Fleck as he fell. Two sets of talons tore at him, and then the birds veered off. He fell, spinning into the water. Battered and cut, he plunged below the surface. After a painful few seconds, he forced his way up and emerged. He looked up and around, surveying the hopeless scene. Pain screamed for his attention, but he pushed it away.

All three ships were engulfed in flames. Chaos reigned on *Lillie's* deck. The attack was concentrated there. He found a net slung over the side, and he climbed, pain screaming with every inch, and at last tumbled onto the deck.

There he saw several knots of fighting rabbits, their swords slicing the air. The deck was littered with the fallen, and in the midst of it stood the king and the prince, fighting for their lives. Around them fought several of the bucks of Black Star Company, including Burnley and Kay Jack. Captain Vance and Joyner were there as well, desperately defending alongside the miners. Burnley swung his massive axe, making contact at times but receiving too many wounds in return. He was a wall before his king and prince, but he was crumbling. King Whitson himself fought hard, keeping Lander between him and the valiant wounded Burnley.

Fleck saw Massie defending poor Gavin near the hatchway. Gavin could barely stand. Massie dealt death with his bow, and Fleck saw that some of the fallen fowl were riddled with arrows. But Massie was running out of arrows, and three birds fell on him at once. Fleck despaired. In a fraction of a second, he considered his awful choices. If he went to the king, no one would be there to help Massie and Gavin.

He ran for Massie.

As he neared them, he leapt onto a pile of ropes and sprang into the air, driving his shoulder into the nearest bird of prey. It knocked sideways into its partner, and both fell askew on deck, momentarily stunned. Fleck fell hard to the deck behind Massie and Gavin. The third bird came for Massie, who drew his sword and made an errant swipe at it. His attacker beat his wings, halting in midair while Massie nearly fell over with his heavy, hapless stroke. The bird beat his wings again and burst onto Massie, clawing him and striking out with his beak. Fleck rose, grabbing a discarded sword from the deck. He dove, sword foremost, and buried it in the bird's shoulder. Screeching with agony, the monster released

Massie, flew sideways over the rail, and crashed into the lake.

Massie was wounded, and Gavin wasn't moving. Fleck glanced at the king, under heavy attack from ten birds as the bucks around him fell one by one. Burnley lay motionless in front of Prince Lander, who was now exposed to attack.

Fleck pushed Gavin to the hatchway.

"Get him below," he ordered Massie. Fleck drove his aching body toward the command deck. He dodged blows from frenzied friends and terrible foes alike and finally came to fill Burnley's spot. Swinging his sword in a wide arc, he beat back the attack of a furious bird bent on snatching the young prince.

Galt was nearby, trying to avoid being killed or snatched by a pair of hideously large birds. Fleck's heart sank when he realized Galt had become like a plaything to them. His fury rose at seeing the friend of his youth, his lieutenant and partner, being so abused. He dropped his sword and reached for Burnley's axe, which now lay on the deck beside the fallen miner. With a tremendous effort, he drew the axe behind his head and hurled it at Galt's two attackers. The axe collided with the foremost, sending him toppling over the side, while the other's expression changed from playful to deadly, and he came at Fleck with such force and speed that the valiant rabbit had no chance. His bloody beak extended, striking Fleck's shoulder and rolling him over painfully. Fleck felt talons fasten on him, heard and felt the whoosh of beating wings. Then the deck grew smaller as he was lifted into the sky.

Fleck fought to stay conscious. He saw that Galt had been grabbed as well. Both were rising over the water in the clutches of hideous birds.

Fleck felt for his sword, but it was not there. He did have a knife, which he strained to reach without effect. He scanned the shrinking deck, looking for any sign of hope. The last thing he saw was Massie standing on deck, wounded but determined, a flame illuminating the tip of a nocked arrow.

Massie was aiming right at Fleck. He let go, and the arrow sped upward, flame stretching thin in flight. Fleck felt it whiz past his face and heard it sink with a hiss into his captor. The suffocating pain of the talon grip eased, then fell away, and Fleck dropped to the water. He had been dropped just short of Dopple's Point.

He could barely breathe. He felt torn in half. He swam for the shore and heard an agonizing screech, followed by two heavy splashes just behind him.

Tales of Old Natalia

Chapter Seventeen

Two soaked and battered rabbits washed up on the shore of Ayman Lake.

Gasping, Fleck crawled onto the stony beach, rolled over, and tried to clear his head.

Galt was already standing. "We have to go, Fleck," he said, eyes darting from the lake to the tree line.

"I'm no traitor," Fleck managed to say through ragged breaths.

"Traitor?" Galt cried. "The winning side gets to decide who the traitors were. We've lost, Fleck. It's over. Even you, Captain Blackstar, can do nothing this time. We have no chance."

"We? *We* have no chance?"

"*He* has no chance," Galt said, head down,

133

edging toward the forest.

Fleck stood slowly, staggering. The usually grey fur of his arm was blotched with dark scarlet. One eye was swollen shut.

"He can be saved," Fleck said, reaching for his sword. His hand closed on air. His scabbard was empty.

"Nothing," Galt said. "There's nothing we can do. It's the end of the world. It's the end of the world!"

"But the oath, Galt. Remember? We can still turn this. King Whitson needs us. Prince Lander needs us," he said, pointing to the burning ship. "I'll never turn traitor."

"You're only a traitor if you betray yourself," Galt said. He sprinted off, disappearing into the trees.

Fleck struggled to stay upright. Swaying, he turned from the fleeing rabbit to face the lake. Charcoal smoke corkscrewed into the sky. The blackened ship teemed with enemies. Flames snapped at the red-diamond standard as the last kingsbucks grappled with the invaders on the deck. Whitson Mariner stood among them, his sword poised and his harried shouts echoing over the lake.

The Black Star of Kingston

Fleck straightened and stretched his arm. Pain flared. Unbearable agony. He bent, wincing.

He opened his eyes and saw King Whitson fighting desperately to protect Prince Lander. Fleck rose, ignoring the pain, and shouted across the water.

"My place beside you, my blood for yours! Till the Green Ember rises, or the end of the world!"

Swordless, Fleck Blackstar hobbled to the water's edge and plunged in.

* * *

After an agonizing swim, he reached *Lillie* and climbed up the net that still hung over the edge of the burning ship. He looked across the water to Seddleton and winced at the flaming ruin it was fast becoming. The enemy's attack now centered on the three ships and primarily on *Lillie*, the largest. But instead of going on deck, where enemies multiplied, he climbed through a porthole and discovered a huddling band of rabbits below deck.

"What are you doing here?" he shouted. "Get on deck now and fight for your king!" Many were shamed and heeded his call, including poor Gavin, who roused himself for a final, futile act of courage. Others slunk into the corners. Fleck searched for a sword but found none. He grabbed a pickaxe from the now-useless supplies he had checked only that morning. He charged for the ladder, pickaxe in hand, and began to climb. But he stopped, hearing the baneful screams from above. He looked back at the supplies.

"Gavin!" he shouted at the rabbit, who was just now reaching the top of the ladder. "Come back!"

"But Captain," Gavin said weakly, "I want to die up there, not down here like a coward."

"Come down at once!"

Gavin obeyed as quickly as he was able.

Fleck climbed the ladder and stuck his head above deck, where chaos, blood, and fire reigned. He couldn't see as far as the command deck, but the latecomers he had roused from below deck had made a small opening in the mass of monsters. Fleck reached for a rolling torch and grabbed one, then disappeared below. He handed Gavin the torch and motioned for him to stand back. Fleck crossed the hold and swung his axe, breaking open a blastpowder barrel and spilling a quantity of the powder along the floor. Then he hurled the barrel into the corner, where it rammed into the other barrels, split, and spilled its powder in a heap.

"Time for fire," he said to Gavin, taking the torch from the weary, smiling rabbit. "Now up top and do what you can. Then over the edge, Gavin."

The frail rabbit nodded and pulled himself up the ladder. When Gavin was through the hatch, Fleck dropped the torch. Flame met powder and sparked to life, racing along the trail toward the large stack of barrels in the corner of the hold.

Fleck was already gone. Emerging from the hatch with a fierce cry, he ran for the command deck. He shouted as he went, his hoarse voice rising over the wild cacophony of battle.

"Burnout! Burnout!" he cried, and the cry was taken up by the few miners left alive on board. "Burnout!" He raced to the command deck and saw, with alarm, that Prince Lander was gone. He spun and searched the sky, but he could not locate the prince. He screamed and turned toward the command deck. The king was surrounded by five laughing monsters, his sword broken in two and his face awash in pain.

Fleck surged ahead, the devastation on deck fueling his boiling rage, intent on only one thing.

He broke through the band of attackers and plowed into the king, carrying him over the side. The birds screeched and struck out madly at the pair, but they were over the rail and falling to the water when it came.

A shattering crack resounded over the lake. The ship came apart in a terrific burst of bright fire. Fleck drove King Whitson down, sheltering him from the countless splintered shards that filled the sky and hit the water like so many arrows. A few found Fleck, and he reeled, at last losing his grip on the king.

He was losing his hold on life. He tried to swim, but his vision blurred, black stars multiplying before his eyes until all was dark and he sank, forgetting everything.

Tales of Old Natalia

Chapter Eighteen

Whitson broke the lake surface and saw that Fleck was sinking. He wasted no time. He dove, his long feet beating as he plunged again into the roiling water. He grabbed Fleck and, with a tremendous effort, drew him back to the surface. Whitson inhaled deeply and took a moment to survey the frenzied scene. He only had a few seconds, but he made several decisions in that moment. *Lillie* was utterly destroyed, and a quarter of *Natalia* had been blown apart. It was listing starboard, and most of its remaining deck was on fire. *Vanguard* was closer to shore, on fire and badly damaged, but the king believed it might be saved. The enemies, those few who had survived, were retreating across the water. None even looked back. A few brave rabbits stood on deck of the ruined *Natalia* and shot volley after volley of arrows at the retreating birds. All this the king saw in the space of three seconds. Then his most pressing concern returned to him in a surge of panic.

Where is Lander?

Wood debris in every shape and size was scattered over the surface of the lake. Rabbits for a half mile rode on the wreckage, trying to make either Dopple's Point or the shore at Seddleton. A few rabbits nearby were holding onto a raft-sized section of the ruined ship, which curved up on the side. Whitson recognized it as the portside hull, reinforced and slick with lake scum. He delivered Captain Blackstar into their care, motioned for them to take him to shore, and swam back toward the burning, bobbing wreckage of *Lillie*, calling as he swam, "Lander! Lander, son!"

He beat at the water, swimming madly into the messiest part of the wreckage, coming up to scan and shout, then diving in again. "Lander!" he cried. Whitson listened for an answer, but he could hardly hear anything. Since the blast, his ears had felt full of sawdust, and they rang with a solitary, ceaseless note.

"Lander! Do you hear me, son?"

Small boats embarked from *Vanguard* and a few from the shore. Their crews dragged haggard rabbits from the red-stained lake. These they returned to the shore, where volunteers did all they could to save and care for the survivors.

The raft bearing Captain Blackstar met with a boat, and after a brief exchange the rabbits on board rowed furiously toward the king.

When they reached him, Whitson was beginning to fade. His weary cries of "Lander, Lander, my son," had fallen to weak and desperate whispers. Lord Grant was at the prow. He ordered the oarsmen to bring the boat alongside the king. They hauled him in, and Lord Grant took off his own large cape and wrapped the king in it.

"Quickly now," he called. "Back to shore."

"Lander," the king called weakly. "My only son."

"Perhaps he's been found, Your Majesty," Lord Grant said, giving the king a drink from a skin, but his worried face told Whitson he had little hope. The blast had saved so many, but many more had lost their lives, and the prince was nowhere to be seen.

In a few minutes the boat reached the shallow shore, and Whitson, somewhat recovered, climbed off the boat. There was wild disorder on shore. Rabbits converged from the ruined town, the battered and blasted ships, and the lake. The lake and shore alike were busy with urgent activity. But several rabbits were still. Motionless soldiers lay along the beach. Soaked sailors, whose ceaseless coughing was strangely reassuring, lay beside them.

Whitson hurried past them. He came to a clustered huddle of nobles, half-burned and bloodied but busy with the task of leading this recovery.

"Your Majesty!" Lord Jaymin called, and the whole group gathered around him, some near tears. "We thought you were lost, sir."

"Where's Lillie?" Whitson asked, sparing them a weary smile. "And Lander? Has he come ashore?"

Lord Jaymin smiled and pointed. The nobles gave way, and a path between them opened. There, sitting on the shore, was Prince Lander. He was wet, of course, but otherwise he looked fine. Queen Lillie knelt beside him, speaking into the ear of what looked like a lifeless rabbit. Whitson ran to them, tears filling his eyes.

Tales of Old Natalia

Chapter Nineteen

Fleck awoke, starting up suddenly, his pulse quickening.

"Relax, Captain," someone said. "The battle is over. You saved us."

Fleck turned to see King Whitson alongside Doctor Grimes, who was forcing a bedraggled white rabbit to drink.

"Gavin!" Fleck said, a smile appearing on his worn and beaten face.

"He'll be all right," Doctor Grimes said. "Just don't get him excited. You might make it as well, if you'll hold still." Fleck closed his eyes. The bright sky and the constant motion of the lake had made his vision blur and his mind swim.

"I'll just lie down," he said, falling back with

a crunch. He groaned. "My back. It feels all …"

"Stabbed up?" King Whitson said. "It should. You shielded me from the blast, and Doctor Grimes just pulled a few sharp chunks of wood out of your poor back. She stitched you up, but you'll want to lie back easier next time."

Fleck nodded, his mind barely able to make sense of what he heard. Then he sat up again, too quickly. "The prince!"

"I'm here, Captain," Prince Lander said, his voice coming from over near Gavin. "I'm just helping Mr. Gavin, then I'll come and see you as soon as ever I can, sir."

Fleck laughed. It was a happy, almost delirious laugh. "Your Royal Highness, I am so graffi-tide … I am show hon-nurd and …" he trailed off as the king slowly lowered him back onto the blanket.

* * *

When Fleck woke again he peered out uneasily from small slits and saw that the prince loomed above him. A bright emerald dangled from Lander's neck. The queen stood behind him, her hands on his shoulders. "Am I dead?" Fleck asked.

"I don't think so," Prince Lander said, kneeling beside him. "I think you're just busted up real good."

"Doctor Grimes says you should be better in a few weeks," the king said, kneeling down beside his son.

"Gavin?"

"Gavin is doing very well," Queen Lillie said, smiling.

"He saved me, you know," Prince Lander said. "Gavin took me off the ship before the blast."

"He did?" Fleck asked, his smile reappearing. "What a very good rabbit Gavin is. I'm honored to be in his company."

"Am I still allowed in Black Star Company?" Prince Lander asked. "Will I get a star patch?"

"Yes, sir," Fleck said. "You shall have one this instant."

Fleck's father's jacket was shredded and bloody and torn all over. He pulled at the sleeve, and it came away easily. The patch was black, surrounded with scarlet. He offered it to the prince.

"Not your father's patch, Fleck," King Whitson said.

"I want him to have it," Fleck said, pressing

it into the prince's hands. "This was my father's patch. He was a hero."

"So you are like your father?" the prince asked, his eyes wide as he reverently received the patch.

"He is," King Whitson said.

"I am," Fleck whispered.

* * *

The funerals were many and sad. King Whitson stood at each graveside in turn, clasping Lander's hand. Burnley, Captain Vance, and many others were laid to rest. Fleck hobbled to each service. It took him a long time to recover, but in time he did. They did not see their enemies again for half a year. By then, much had changed.

Fleck took Burnley's black star patch for his own. It went on his shoulder on a new coat made by Queen Lillie herself. A black star also adorned the tunic she made for him, serving as the sign of his coat of arms.

King Whitson had made him a lord.

* * *

Whitson was more active than ever. His heroic reputation grew, and the community found a way to recover after the calamitous attack of Ayman Lake. Fleck stayed behind when the king led most of the community west in search of a new home. It was hard for King Whitson to leave Seddleton. But it was a ruin, and he knew they needed to press farther into Natalia, away from the High Bleaks. Fleck had a writ from Whitson stating he was to command the mine and build a deep, secure warren nearby. Lord Blackstar was charged with defense and industry in the place he named Kingston. The mine was called Burnley's Colliery.

Gavin stayed. Hollis stayed. Brephen, Kay Jack, and the other survivors of Black Star Company stayed, along with more brave families intent on building a new community. Massie was asked to travel with the king and, when they reached their final home, to return to Kingston with news of where the main body of rabbits had settled.

Fleck had wanted to go, to stay with the king and his family and to defend them always. But Whitson now believed it was too dangerous for them all to remain in only one company. Had it not been for Fleck's heroics, the Battle of Ayman

Lake could have wiped them all out. So he appointed Fleck as Lord Blackstar and charged him and his rabbits to build a new community. The community at Kingston would long remember the way the king left and what he said when they sailed away.

* * *

King Whitson stood on the command deck of *Vanguard*, Lander at his side. The entire ship's crew stood at attention along the rails. Captain Walters cried, "Pass the word for silence! The king will speak."

There was no need for this order. No one moved, let alone dared talk. King Whitson stood at the rail, his crown glittering in the sunlight. On the shore Lord Blackstar knelt, along with every member of his community, Gavin at his side.

Whitson called across the water. "Fleck, my friend!"

"My king!" Fleck called; then he fell silent.

The king spoke again, shouting across the water. "My place beside you. My blood for yours. Till the Green Ember rises, or the end of the world!"

Epilogue

Whitson Mariner embarked on many more adventures, and these are recorded in the *Tales of Old Natalia*. But he never forgot Captain Blackstar, and he made certain that Fleck's memory lived on. Every year, upon the anniversary of the battle, Whitson would remind his subjects of what Fleck had done. He would especially recount those deeds to Prince Lander and the other youngsters. Rabbit children through the following decades, from Ayman Lake to the eventual site of First Warren and beyond, heard stories of bravery. They heard stories to make them brave.

They heard tales of the Black Star of Kingston. And with those tales came Blackstar's oath, often repeated, so that it became the creed of all those loyal to Whitson and his line.

"My place beside you. My blood for yours. Till the Green Ember rises, or the end of the world!"

The End

About the Author

In seventh grade, S. D. "Sam" Smith moved from his beloved West Virginia to Africa. He turned thirteen years old in South Africa the day Nelson Mandela was released from prison. Years later, when Sam and his family left their adopted home country, Mandela was the president. Life is, as the man who loves cliches once said, a story. And S. D. Smith has lived a fairly interesting one so far. He loves to invite kids to see that, while they may not be the author of their story, they are characters who are able to make choices, take action, and change the story.

Sam now lives in Grandview, West Virginia, with his wife, Gina, and their four children. The Smiths love to cook out, play soccer, garden, create stories, watch (and listen to) birds, draw, read books, play music, and generally enjoy the many wonders of creation.

www.SDSmith.net

About the Illustrator

In seventh grade, a kid sitting behind Zach Franzen in music class reached into a ziplock bag of pencil bits and hurled some pieces at his head. Zach whipped around and threw his pen at the assailant. It turned once in the air and stuck in the boy's forehead. This is a true story. An onlooker, desiring to confirm what he witnessed, repeated, "It stuck in his head." These days Zach seeks to use his pen, pencil, or brush to create images. Hopefully, these images might have force enough to stick in the heads of those who see them.

Zach lives in Greenville, South Carolina, with his wife, Alissa, and their daughters. The Franzens love to drink tea, read stories, sing harmonies, perform in plays, paint, eat (but not eat paint), and take walks so they can say Hi to all the dogs in the neighborhood.

www.AtoZach.com

About the Illustrator

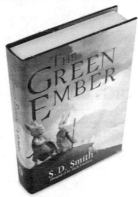
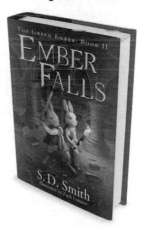

Keep up with author S. D. Smith

Sign up for his funny, infrequent newsletter for good deals, news about upcoming books, and more.

www.sdsmith.net/updates

If you loved the book, please give it a review online now. Positive reviews help so much. Thank you.